# BEATLES, BOLT HOLES, AND VIDEO NASTIES

## arthur burke

coffeetownpress

Kenmore, WA

coffeetown**press**

A Coffeetown Press book published by Epicenter Press

Epicenter Press
6524 NE 181st St.
Suite 2
Kenmore, WA 98028

For more information go to:
www.Camelpress.com
www.Coffeetownpress.com
www.Epicenterpress.com
www.arthurburkebooks.com

This is a work of fiction. Names, characters, places, brands, media, and incidents are either the product of the author's imagination or are used fictiously.

Cover design by Scott Book
Design by Melissa Vail Coffman

*Beatles, Bolt Holes, and Video Nasties*
Copyright © 2024 by Arthur Burke

Library of Congress Control Number: 2023951891

ISBN: 978-1-68492-185-0 (Trade Paper)
ISBN: 978-1-68492-186-7 (eBook)

# Acknowledgments

MY THANKS TO LISA AND EDMUND, who read early drafts of this book and made many useful suggestions, and to Phil Garrett and Jennifer McCord at Epicenter Press for their continuing support.

# CHAPTER ONE

I WAS IN MY PUSHCHAIR AT AN OPEN-AIR MARKET. The old man at the fruit stall put some green grapes into my hand and I let them fall to the ground. A woman's voice behind me said, "Sorry, he's a fussy eater, this one. He gets it from his dad." That must have been my mother. Apart from that, I have no memories of her. I didn't hear raised voices or slamming doors. There was no Bambi moment when I was told my mother couldn't be with me anymore. It was just me and my dad in the house. I've never blamed her for leaving. Being married to my dad can't have been easy. He was an academic, whose subject was modern history. He came alive when sharing insights into why Churchill lost the 1945 election but stammered and wheezed when expected to express emotion. He knew the date of every event in World War Two but never remembered birthdays or anniversaries.

He talked about my mother occasionally and I pieced together their story. They met at university. I only have his word for it, but it seems he was the star of the history department. He published papers in *The Journal of Contemporary History* while still a fresher. By his final year, lecturers stood aside and let him teach the class. He stayed up all night in his room working on dissertations. My mother stayed up all night in the student union bar watching The

Who and The Pink Floyd. A lot of eyebrows were raised when she got together with my dad. Her friends expected her to hook up with some stoner dude who played in a band. I've seen photos of her. She was tall, pencil thin, with long brown hair and large dark eyes, highlighted by copious black eyeliner. She dressed in the 1960s student chic of black sweater and brown corduroy trousers. My dad was short and plump with uncombed sandy hair. He usually had a reddish-blond beard, not because he liked the hippie look but because he couldn't be bothered to shave most days. Unfortunately, that recessive gene pushed its way to the front, and I take after him with my dirty blond hair. I don't dare grow a beard in case it comes out ginger. As a student, my dad always wore a white shirt with a thin greasy-looking black tie and baggy grey trousers. There were mutters my mother was out of his league, but his intensity when expounding his views gave him a mesmeric charisma. Even though she was reading English literature, she spent hours with my dad, listening to him talk about history. After he'd told her the sixth reason why the Spanish Civil War was inevitable, she could resist no longer and kissed him. They married quickly but she soon realised what should have been obvious from the start. The love of his life was history and no one was going to change that. They had me as a last-ditch attempt at saving their relationship. Maybe she hoped the needs of a baby would force my dad away from his books. I was born on 22 November 1968. It was becoming fashionable for fathers to attend the birth. My dad was happy to get out of this as my mother insisted that he go and buy a copy of The Beatles' *White Album*, which came out on the same day I did.

I failed in my job to rescue their marriage and my mother walked out before my fourth birthday. When I say that, people tell me how awful my childhood must have been, but you don't miss what you don't remember, and the children at school often made mothers sound like a malevolent force. If a kid got a bad mark or ripped a hole in his shirt, the standard wail was, "My mum will kill me!" I never feared for my life. My shirt could have been on fire and my dad wouldn't have noticed. He cared about education, though, and always helped me when I was struggling with a subject. As he explained a point to me, I understood what my mother had seen in him. He was a riveting teacher. Even when the subject wasn't history, he had a passion for making a point understood. "Look at my watch," he said, holding his wrist an inch from my face. "How does it work? Electricity from the battery makes the quartz crystal pulsate at a precise frequency, so the watch records the passing of time, accurate to plus or minus one second a day. A similar thing happens in your heart. The right atrium has something called the sinoatrial node. Here, I'll write that down for you. It generates an electrical impulse which causes the walls of the atria to contract, forcing blood into the ventricles. Do you understand? Explain it to me, using different words." As soon as he was sure I did understand, the fire went out of his eyes, and he went back to his own work.

Someone like him could never have survived in a regular job. He wouldn't have been able to hide his boredom during meetings or his contempt for the boss. Fortunately, the impressive list of papers he'd published as an undergraduate served him well and he was given the first academic post he applied for. Only a hotbed of eccentricity like a university would tolerate someone who shambled in wearing the clothes he'd had on for the last three days and fell asleep at his desk as soon as people stopped asking him questions. If my dad had a boss, it was Professor Pearce. He knew better than to involve my dad in departmental politics. If they passed each other in the corridor, the professor would ask, "Content or not content?"

My dad always replied, "Content," and Professor Pearce walked on, happy with his people management skills.

I know about this because my dad took me into the university when he thought the lecture he was giving would interest me. I sat at the back. A couple of students speculated I might be a child genius and I was in no hurry to disabuse them. I doubt it occurred to them I was the lecturer's son: my dad didn't look the type to procreate. He was popular with the students. His passion for the subject made his lectures more interesting than most. He was always ready to talk to someone with a genuine interest in history. One female student remarked he was least creepy don on campus. Faced with a beautiful woman, he'd always choose a discussion of decolonization over making a pass at her.

The students had learned to recognise when the lecture was coming to an end. As soon as my dad started to roll a cigarette, they gathered their pens and papers together. A knot of students stood around with him afterwards. He often went through three cigarettes clarifying and expanding on the points he'd made. I was as enthralled as they were. After they'd left, he gave me a signal and we went home.

We lived in an Edwardian six-bedroom detached house. If you think that sounds grand for a university lecturer, you're right. My parents got it at a knockdown price because it was so dilapidated. A family of five had bought it in the early years of the twentieth century. Shortly after the children had left home, the husband died, leaving the widow alone. She shrank her world down to the front room, sleeping in an armchair and heating up soup on a camping stove in the corner. She only ventured out of the room to go to the shops or use the bathroom. For the next thirty years, the rest of the house fell into disrepair. After she died, the children put the house on the market. Most people took one look and walked away, seeing too much work. My mother, on the other hand, saw a project. Maybe this was the other part of her scheme to save the marriage. She and my dad would bond over renovating a house together. It was no more successful than her plan to have me. She walked out long before finishing the job, which she'd been doing by herself. She'd decorated the front room with cream wallpaper and a deep brown carpet. If I lifted one corner of it, I saw the blackened floorboards where the old lady's camping stove had been. I did this at least once a day. There was a thrilling chill to seeing traces of the dead woman.

My bedroom was the gift my mother gave me before she left. I've no idea if she intended it that way. It had a citrus brightness with its yellow-painted walls and green curtains. I was most grateful for the thick green carpet. I spent hours lying on it, listening to music.

She never got round to decorating the master bedroom. Its walls were bare, cracked plaster. A single unshaded lightbulb hung from the middle of the ceiling. My dad didn't care because he never spent any conscious time in there. Refusing to be bound by what he called the tyranny of the clock, he worked at the dining room table until he couldn't keep his eyes open. If he was inspired to write at three in the morning, that's what he did. He often fell asleep in his chair. If he made it up the stairs, it was touch and go whether he managed to change into his pyjamas. More often than not, he lay diagonally across the bed, fully dressed. If you'd asked him what colour the curtains in his bedroom were, he wouldn't have known.

The other rooms had remained untouched for years. The old lady's children had taken all the valuables but left a lot of other stuff behind. Wardrobes loomed menacingly in dim corners. I could stare at one for an hour before having the courage to open the door. In my mind, they led to secret passages or contained time capsules of bygone ages. The reality was never so interesting. There were some old clothes, which I put on. Could I pass for a grown-up with a man's coat pulled up high and his Panama hat pulled down low? I tried on a couple of dresses but wasn't thrilled with either the look or feel, so decided not to be a transvestite. I was convinced the long shadowy landing and dark rooms were haunted. The spirit of the old lady prowled around, unhappy about these strangers in her house. I never saw her, but a window frame rattling, or a floorboard creaking sounded exactly like the footsteps of a restless spirit.

On my own for most of the time, I invented people to accompany me in exploring the house. I was the headmaster of a school for the gifted and led a small group of my pupils on a tour around this fascinating old house. I explained points of architectural or historical interest quietly but out loud. They hung upon my every word, which I liked. I sometimes thought I'd prefer to have real people to talk to, but I decided they might disagree with me or have their own ideas about what they wanted to do. That would be just wrong.

There was a moment every evening when the walls and ceiling closed in. My pupils' voices faded into silence, and I was no longer an inspirational teacher. I was a small, pale boy alone in a dark room in a big, old house. When this happened, I went to join my dad in the dining room. He didn't mind so long as I didn't interrupt his work. Sitting at the table with him, I pretended to read or do my homework. Really, I was watching him. As he wrote, he muttered to himself, "What is this about? Does that follow?" Occasionally, he paused and frowned. "Am I being an idiot?" he asked aloud. This was followed either with a relieved look or by screwing up the sheet of paper and adding it to the pile around the bin. He read a history book like he was watching a football match. An excited "Yes!" before a despairing groan meant the author had made a promising point before coming to the wrong conclusion. "Yes! Yes! Oh, yes!" was his equivalent of, "He shoots! He scores!" and meant the author had come up with an important new insight.

Being with him for an hour made the house less scary. My students started talking to me again and we went upstairs to listen to some music. They were always impressed by my choices and appreciated my analysis of the songs.

When my dad didn't make it to bed at all, he had a shower and two strong coffees before going into work. After getting through whatever lectures and seminars he had that day, he slept in his room at the university or came home and went to bed. He didn't impose any tyranny of the clock on me either. I often fell asleep on my bedroom floor in front of the vinyl record player and woke to the rhythmic click of the stylus going round and round an album's inner groove. Meals were equally haphazard. Occasionally, my dad would put something in the oven, go back to his books, then wonder what the burning smell was. Otherwise, his research was fuelled by cigarettes, black coffee, cornflakes, and chocolate. He bought these at the tuck shop on campus. There was always enough for me too. I never went hungry, but it wasn't the healthiest diet. The lack of fruit and vegetables gave me constipation often lasting a week. It was uncomfortable, but I was happy to be spared the indignity of going to the toilet. I saw my life as a blend of the aesthetic and intellectual, with my appreciation of music, my insights into history, and my scholarly analyses of films. Something as crudely animalistic as shitting was repugnant to me. Every six weeks or so, my body protested by giving me stomach cramps so severe all I could do was curl up in bed. I don't know if my dad suffered from his eating habits. If he ever got sick, he did what he always did when faced with something unpleasant. He ignored it and carried on working.

If I asked my dad to tell me a story, he pointed out that story was five sevenths of history and talked me through the major events of the twentieth century. The villains I heard about were not the Evil Queen or the Big Bad Wolf, but Hitler and Stalin. My dad didn't see any reason to dumb down and spoke to me like I was a meeting of the Royal Historical Society. This caused issues when I went to school. There aren't many five-year-olds who talk about historical objectivity or the values of the Enlightenment. The other children didn't bully me much but treated me like I was one of the foreign kids they didn't understand and left me alone. The fug of cigarette smoke hanging around our house gave me a persistent cough, so the teachers were happy for me to stay in and read during break times instead of braving the outdoors. This spared me the embarrassment of sitting on my own in a corner of the playground, trying to look fascinated by a passing ant. Part of me would have liked to play French cricket or dodgeball with the others, but I didn't know how to get into the game. I could discuss the competing advantages of primary and secondary historical sources, but didn't know the words, "Can I play, please?"

I didn't normally envy the other children. They were force fed vegetables and sent to bed at eight o'clock. I did sometimes feel sad on Monday mornings. We started the school week by writing a diary on what we'd done over the weekend, which we read out to the class. From the age of nine, I spent every weekend listening to records, so my diary took the form of an album review. "Having used up most of their new songs on *A Hard Day's Night*, the group fell back on under-inspired cover versions for their follow-up, *Beatles For Sale*. 'Mr Moonlight' and 'Honey Don't' are unlikely to make many people's list of favourite Beatles' songs." This wasn't what the teachers wanted to hear, but they felt sorry for me, so didn't complain too much. The other kids would read out things like, "I played football in the garden with my dad," or "Daddy took us to the park." I once asked my dad if he'd take me to the park. He frowned and said, "What good would that do?" I had no answer, so didn't ask again. I figured I was more of a pet hamster to him than a dog. He wanted me to be safe and he kept me fed, but he didn't play games with me or take me for a walk.

Speaking of pets, there was one time I wished he could have been more of a regular dad. When I was ten, Aunty Joy, my dad's sister, bought me a rabbit. He was black, so my dad suggested calling him Oswald, after the famously black-shirted Mosley. It was odd, naming a cute bunny after a notorious fascist, but somehow it suited him. Oswald sat beside me, meditatively chewing a lettuce leaf, and we listened to albums together. A heavy drum break would send him hopping behind the wardrobe, but otherwise he seemed to like the music and I enjoyed his company. Unfortunately, he fell victim to flystrike two years later. After burying Oswald in the garden, I asked my dad if rabbits went to heaven. The correct response was, "Yes, of course they do. Oswald's up there now, having a great time." My dad rolled a cigarette, signifying a lengthy answer on the way. "If you had a powerful enough telescope, you could see Neptune and Pluto. How big a telescope would you need to see heaven?"

I was still too upset about my pet to give much thought to astronomy. "I don't know."

"No telescope will ever let you see heaven. No spacecraft will send back pictures from the celestial surface. We're supposed to believe a mysterious portal opens at the moment of death and we're transported into some alternate dimension. Everyone who has ever existed will be there, providing they've passed some entrance exam based on how they lived their lives. For those who fail the exam, this loving and compassionate God has devised an eternal torture chamber full of excruciating punishments. Many of these people were put in the ground decades, centuries ago. Their bodies have decayed until there is nothing left of them, but now they're walking around again. What do you think you're going to do in heaven? Join a thousand-year long queue to meet Julius Caesar or Shakespeare?" He paused and took a drag on his cigarette. "I ask you, how likely does any of that sound?"

At twelve years old, I didn't understand the finer points of my father's eschatology but went away thinking Oswald wasn't in leporine paradise eating carrot ambrosia.

# CHAPTER TWO

T HERE WAS ONE NIGHT NEITHER OF US WENT TO BED—Thursday
3 May 1979, election day. Before any results were announced,
my dad was already on the edge of his seat, looking for some crumb
of comfort in what the pundits were saying. Maybe the British people had come to their senses in the privacy of the voting booth
and defied the opinion polls. With cigarette and coffee cup full of
whiskey in hand, my dad became more and more anxious as all the
indications pointed to only one result. I was bored by the specula-
tion and wanted to sleep, but I saw how important this was to my
dad and I was determined to support him. With Coke and chocolate biscuits as my substitute for whiskey and cigarettes, I sat up all
night and saw the results coming in. By four in the morning, there
was no doubt what the outcome would be. We were still watching
as the sun came up. If my dad remembered I was supposed to be
in school, he didn't care. He remained tense and nervous, but there
was a tiny gleam in his eye until Mrs Thatcher arrived at Downing
Street and announced, "Her Majesty the Queen has asked me to
form a new administration and I have accepted." My dad slumped
back in his chair, tears rolling down his face. I'd never seen him cry
before. Slowly and deliberately, he said, "We are fucked." I'd never
heard him use language like that, either. He'd been clinging to a

forlorn hope that the Queen would exercise her prerogative and save the country from Thatcher. He of all people knew it would trigger an almighty constitutional crisis if the Queen tried to overturn an election result, but it was the only straw he had to clutch. When Mrs Thatcher started quoting Saint Francis of Assisi, "Where there is discord, may we bring harmony . . ." my dad sprang to his feet and looked on the point of kicking in the television screen. Wiser counsels prevailed and he settled for turning it off.

He despised Mrs Thatcher's policies of dismantling the welfare state and castrating the unions, but he also had a more personal reason for fearing her. During her time as Education Secretary, she'd used one of her favourite expressions, 'market forces,' when allocating research funding. It highlighted a fundamental difference between her and my dad. He would have given the money to whatever research looked most interesting, regardless of whether anyone stood to get rich off it. For him, education was an end in itself. The human mind was a wonderful thing so why wouldn't you stretch it to the limit by cramming it with history, literature, science, or whatever your interest was? The idea of learning as nothing more than gaining a professional qualification was like keeping a great painting in a vault and treating it as an investment. He saw a university as a place where youngsters went to grow and explore new ideas. Mrs Thatcher saw it as a training centre where people learned how to do a job. Departments of medicine, law, and engineering felt secure. Those of English literature, philosophy, and history were more precarious.

After switching off the TV, my dad turned around and stumbled. Half a bottle of whiskey had disappeared during the night. He wasn't normally much of a drinker. "I'm going to sleep," he said, bleakly. "Wake me up when she resigns." He didn't know that would mean staying in bed for the next eleven years.

# CHAPTER THREE

ONCE A FORTNIGHT, MY DAD TOOK A FEW HOURS off work to indulge his other interest, which was classic films. On Sunday evening, he took me into town on the bus. We walked down an alleyway between a multi-storey car park and a gentlemen's outfitter. There was a pub at the end of the alley, which was rumoured to have a twenty-four-hour police watch on account of all the fights and drug deals that went down. A low whitewashed building with a black door squatted next to it. 'FORUM' was painted on the door in gold letters. My dad and I were greeted by Mr Brownlow, a man in his forties with curly black hair, a bushy moustache, and thick round glasses. He always looked pleased to see us and talked about how he'd managed to track down the film we were about to see. A contact in France or Italy had sent him a lost gem by Robert Bresson or Vittorio De Sica. An American seaman had brought over a print of a John Ford film, with an extra three seconds never previously seen in Britain.

My dad paid 50p for his ticket and 25p for mine. The price included a drink. I never saw any alcohol there, but Mr Brownlow had installed a kettle and a soft drinks dispenser behind the tiny bar. He made a black coffee for my dad and gave me a large plastic cup of Coke. I always preferred Coke from the machine. It wasn't as fizzy as the stuff from a can and had a better flavour. If we were lucky, there was also a cardboard box full of chocolate bars. The seats in the auditorium varied in size and colour. Mr Brownlow had rescued some from a local theatre that had closed. Others, he'd bought at flea markets. Our favourites were two blue armchairs at the back of the room. We sank into those with a chocolate bar on the arm between us and watched the film. I didn't always understand what was happening onscreen and I shouldn't have been seeing films like *Psycho* and *The Cabinet of Dr Caligari* from the age of four. This early exposure to horror films might explain my later fascination with video nasties. It was always the same group of people at the screenings. I was the only child. After the film ended, everyone stayed in the auditorium, talking about the film over more coffee and endless cigarettes. The discussion was often twice as long as the film itself. The acting, script, directorial choices, lighting, and soundtrack were all dissected. This was why I never had nightmares after watching horror films. If I saw someone murdered on the screen, I wasn't frightened. I was too busy analysing the use of special effects, music, and editing. I contributed my opinions. The other people frequently disagreed with what I said. Looking back, I see it was a huge compliment they thought it worth arguing with me. It would have been easy for them to exchange patronizing smiles at the little boy who tried to join in the adults' conversation. While they were respectful of my opinions, they were in awe of every word from my dad. He researched classic films with the intellectual rigour he brought to his work, never making a point unless he could back it up with concrete examples. This, coupled with his compelling delivery, had them all leaning forward whenever he spoke. My dad never went to the pub or played golf like other fathers. These people were the closest thing he had to friends.

The beginning of the end for our trips to the Forum came in 1982 after my dad arrived back from the university, sweating under the weight of a huge cardboard box. The history department had invested in a couple of new-fangled machines called video cassette players but found it only needed one. Rather than let the spare one gather dust in a cupboard, my dad brought it home. He had no patience with instruction manuals so stuck cables into promising-looking holes until a picture appeared on the TV screen. The tape he'd brought as a tester was twenty minutes of a dull young man discussing the English Civil War. We watched for a while. It wasn't my dad's preferred historical period so, after he'd gone off to read something more to his taste, I enjoyed making the young man pause mid-sentence, speak at double speed, and do his talk backwards. That was only entertaining for half an hour. We would need other things to watch. My dad had heard a couple of people at the Forum talking about a place ten minutes' walk away called Abdul's Videos.

I didn't pay much attention to Abdul himself on our first visit. I was too enthralled by the surroundings. The first thing to hit me was the shop's smell. I can't say I *liked* the petro-chemical smell of video cassettes, but it was the scent of freedom. It's hard for people today to appreciate what dizzying possibilities were offered by the arrival of home video. Before, if you wanted to see a movie after it had left the cinemas, you either had to belong to a film society like the Forum or wait for it to be shown on TV. You watched it at the time scheduled by the network and if you missed it, you missed it. There were no options for watching it later. You might have to wait a couple of years before the channel decided to show it again. The idea of being able to watch something *any time you wanted* was bizarre and wonderful.

Abdul had shelves full of films by Frank Capra, Howard Hawks, and George Cukor. My dad saw one he wanted to watch, then immediately saw one he wanted to watch more and filled his arms with them until Abdul pointed out there was a limit of two tapes per visit. My dad was distraught at having to whittle all these great films down to two until Abdul reminded him he could come back as often as he liked. We ended up renting *The Seventh Seal* and *The Bicycle Thieves* for 50p each.

I also saw my first video nasty box cover. It was before the furore kicked off, so I didn't know anything about them. The *Daily Mail* wouldn't begin its campaign to ban the nasties until the following year. Nevertheless, I was drawn to a tape called *Cannibal Ferox*. There were no illustrations on the front of the box, the implication being that every frame of the film was so unspeakably violent not one of them could be shown without outraging public decency. While my dad was talking to Abdul, I snuck a peak at the back cover, where there were some stills from the film. There was nothing too horrendous in them. Their main aim was to assure potential viewers that actress Zora Kerova showed her breasts. I was also interested in the film's self-imposed double-X certificate. Many of the porn videos on the top shelf proudly trumpeted that they were triple-X. I came away with the idea that *Cannibal Ferox* was only twice as shocking as *The Godfather* while *Girls in Uniform* was three times as bad.

Now my dad had a way of indulging his interest in classic films from the comfort of his own home, our Sunday evening trips became rarer until they stopped altogether. If my dad missed Mr Brownlow or the others at the Forum, he never let on.

# CHAPTER FOUR

MY DAD HAD FILMS. I HAD MUSIC. For the first eight years of my life, well-meaning aunts bought me Disney soundtracks and albums by The Wombles. There was nothing wrong with that. I still think 'Bare Necessities' and 'Remember You're a Womble' are good songs. My Keats moment happened when I was nine years old in a music lesson at school. The music teacher had left in the middle of term without bothering to work her notice period. They couldn't find a replacement to start immediately so the history teacher reluctantly took over her lessons. He didn't sing or play any instruments, so there was a limit to how much he could tell us about making music. He fell back on what he knew and taught us the history of music. After weeks of taking us through the medieval, renaissance, baroque, and romantic periods, he finally admitted in the last lesson of term that such things as jazz and pop music existed. The last thing he played us was the chorus of 'Lucy in the Sky with Diamonds.' That was when a new planet swam into my ken. I could not get it out of my head. As I didn't know how the rest of the song went, the single line chorus played on a loop in my mind for the rest of the day. The eighteen second clip was enough to tell me this was a different order of music from anything I'd listened to before.

I couldn't wait to get home that afternoon. One of the rooms upstairs housed the stuff my mother had left behind. Maybe she'd had some notion of coming back to pick it up but never got round to it. Her tie-dyed t-shirts and patchwork jackets were crammed into plastic bags. Most of her books were cheaply produced tracts calling for Western troops to pull out of Vietnam or for Enoch Powell to be arrested as an enemy of mankind. She also had some crime books of the Agatha Christie and Dorothy L. Sayers type, which I read, but kept hidden under my bed because I knew my dad wouldn't approve. I'd seen my mother's music collection before but hadn't paid much attention to it. I'd assumed her records were like the political stuff—artefacts from a bygone age which wouldn't mean anything to me. Now I looked through them with a new interest. She had albums by The Kinks, The Rolling Stones, Simon and Garfunkel, The Who, The Doors, Pink Floyd, The Moody Blues. . .Crucially, she had every record The Beatles ever made. They were all in two big cardboard boxes, which I dragged into my own room. The record player I had must have been my mother's as well. I can't imagine my dad ever owning one. It was a square black box with a single speaker at the front. There were two knobs marked volume and tone. I never noticed any difference no matter how much I turned the tone knob. I found the song I was looking for—side one, track three on something called *Sergeant Pepper's Lonely Hearts Club Band*. I listened to the whole of 'Lucy in the Sky with Diamonds' for the first time. Whether the song is about drugs or not—I'm not getting into that debate here—it took me on a psychedelic trip. I lay on my bedroom floor gazing up at the white ceiling and saw marmalade skies and plasticine porters. When I sat up and tried to listen critically instead of just letting it transport me, I was pulled in a new way every time. The vocals, organ, guitar, and bass were all moving in subtly different directions. Each one sounded interesting enough to be an instrumental in its own right. I couldn't get over how much was going on in every moment of the music.

For more than a week, I played this one song over and over. I don't know if my dad heard it, but he never complained. I lay with my ear three inches from the speaker so I didn't have to play it loud. On a whim one day, I played the rest of the album and started to understand what music could do. The experiments with everything from plucking piano strings with fingers to playing a comb and tissue paper created sounds I'd never heard before. This was coupled with four musicians who perfectly understood how to play together and still wanted to work as a unit.

For months, I listened to nothing except The Beatles. In a world where they existed, why would I listen to anyone else? Every time I played one of their later era songs, I heard something new, so there was no danger of getting bored. In time, I branched out. The Rolling Stones sounded simplistic by comparison when I listened to early songs like 'Come On' or 'Not Fade Away.' By the time of 'Sympathy for the Devil' and 'Gimme Shelter,' they were almost as good as The Beatles at creating soundscapes.

My dad never tried to stop me playing his ex-wife's records. I say 'ex-wife,' but I don't know if they ever went through the formality of getting divorced. It's unusual not to know your parents' marital status, but it's not something my dad ever mentioned. My mother would have found it difficult to get him to agree to a divorce. He hardly ever opened his mail unless the envelope bore the insignia of a prestigious academic institution, so he'd have ignored any letters from lawyers. My guess is she rode it out until she could declare herself a free woman with or without his consent. My dad didn't complain about my music distracting him while he was working. Nevertheless, I told him he could solve this problem by giving me some money to buy a pair of headphones. He found it easier to hand over a ten-pound note than to protest there wasn't a problem in the first place. I chose a pair of bulky black headphones with padded earpieces. I loved them. They became my ultimate bolt hole. With them on, I could disappear completely into the music.

In one of the rooms, I found a small black and white TV. I was surprised to find it still worked. When not listening to music, I watched *The Goodies, Not The Nine O'clock News,* and other programmes my dad would never have on the big television downstairs. He didn't like comedy shows. He had a sense of humour and often made his students laugh. His impression of Mussolini trying to address German troops in their own language was so popular that students requested it, even in lectures that had nothing to do with Mussolini. My dad was good at seeing the comedy in real life. What he had no patience for was people *trying* to be funny. I loved these programmes and watched them obsessively. I learned my favourite sketches by heart and got annoyed when kids at school misquoted them.

I read my dad's history books. He found the real world more interesting than made-up ones so didn't read a lot of fiction. There are certain classic novels every educated person must have read, so he had old hardback copies of them. I enjoyed the epic sweep of Dickens. I suspect, if he were around today, he'd be writing doorstep blockbusters for people to read on the beach. He'd count his millions while the critics derided him. I struggled with Jane Austen until it clicked that she knew how ridiculous and petty-minded the concerns of her characters were. I enjoyed her as soon as I detected the sneer in her voice.

What I most wanted to read about, though, was pop music. My dad had the *Times* and the *Guardian* delivered every morning. He espoused the liberal views of the *Guardian* but also wanted to keep abreast of what the enemy was saying. I walked to the newsagent's and asked if the *Melody Maker* and *New Musical Express* could be added to the order. The girl behind the counter didn't question my authority. She opened the ledger at our address and wrote down the titles. My dad never noticed. I played the good boy when the papers arrived, going to fetch them for my father. It was easy to secrete a music paper somewhere and ferry it up to my room when he wasn't looking. For him, bills were irritants to be dispatched and forgotten rather than studied, so he didn't question why the paper shop was charging a bit extra.

He never remembered my birthday and was always surprised when the twenty-fifth of December turned out to be Christmas Day, so I never expected any presents from him. If the well-meaning aunts asked me what I wanted, I gave them a list of albums or books about music. Soon, my knowledge of John Lennon's life matched my dad's on the career of Josef Stalin. He knew everything about the conflict between Churchill and Lord Halifax. I knew the ins and outs of the feud between Ray and Dave Davies.

It wasn't a normal childhood, but reasonably happy. I was on my own for most of the time, but I had music and TV to keep me company. It was reassuring to know my dad was downstairs even if he was absorbed in something else. I had a soft carpet to lie on, chocolate to eat, interesting things to listen to and read. To paraphrase a wiser man than myself, I was sure nothing was going to change my world.

# CHAPTER FIVE

**W**HEN I WAS TWELVE, IT WAS TIME TO THINK ABOUT a new school. One evening while I was in my room listening to The Rolling Stones' *Aftermath*, my dad put his head round the door and handed me the prospectus of a school which might be a good place for me. I won't mention the school's name in case they sue. It was a ten-minute walk away from our house. I'd gone past it but hadn't taken any notice. No lightning flashes or howling wolves had warned me about the place. The prospectus proudly trumpeted that it was a Quaker school. I wasn't entirely sure what Quakers were. The only ones I'd seen were portly, American gentlemen in broad-brimmed hats on cereal packets. I'd never heard of Quakerism in Britain.

One thing I did know is that it's a religion and I didn't understand why my dad would suggest a religious school for me. In his studies of history, he saw human actions and their consequences. Major events were set in train by a monarch, politician, or military leader. Even so-called acts of God such as floods and earthquakes could be explained with reference to natural phenomena. My dad didn't see the hand of God anywhere. He admitted there was some evidence of a Galilean cult leader called Yahshua, Joshua, or possibly Jesus, but accounts of his words and deeds were clearly mythmaking rather than history. My dad despised religious belief as cowardly reluctance to accept we're nothing more than accidents of nature in a world where random things happen. One thing he detested more than religion, however, was militarism. He would never say he supported the troops but not the war because he loathed them both equally. He had contempt for soldiers who obeyed orders without questioning the rights or wrongs. He believed if a sufficient number of German officers had refused to follow the commands of a jumped-up corporal, the Second World War could have been avoided. I think he's being unfair in this. I've seen enough documentaries about life in the military to know sergeants do not say, "Right, men, we've received our orders. Let's talk them over and see if we feel comfortable obeying them." The advantage of a Quaker school from my dad's point of view was it didn't have an officers' training corps. I liked that too but, for me, a bigger selling point was it didn't have corporal punishment. In the early 1980s, it was considered the height of soggy liberalism to suggest there was anything wrong in hitting children with sticks to make them behave. It was banned in state-run schools in 1986, but parents could pay to have their offspring beaten in private schools until 1998. I hated it. I know it was supposed to be hateful, but it wasn't the pain so much as the violation of my personal space. Someone touching me without my consent was abuse. Spanking and caning belong in the bedrooms of adults who enjoy that sort of thing, not in the classroom. If Quakers felt that way too, I was happy to go along with them.

I asked my dad for a book about Quakers. He'd have felt dirty going into the religion section of the university library, so he found me a book on the history of Quakerism. As I read, I found more to admire about them. They opposed slavery at a time when many people accepted it as a natural part of life. They were also early advocates for women's rights and prison reform. I discovered the Cadbury family were prominent Quakers and I was grateful to them for all the chocolate. I agreed with both my dad and the

Quakers in their total opposition to war. I wasn't waving a flag when British troops went off to fight in the Falkland Islands. The TV news showed the anguished words of a young pregnant woman whose husband was heading off to war, "We thought the Army was a nice, steady job. We had no idea he'd actually have to fight." Her face stayed in my mind and I hoped her husband was all right. Two hundred and fifty-five British troops were killed in the Falklands conflict, fewer than in the first five minutes of the Somme. I couldn't help thinking every one of those young men had someone hoping he'd come home safely. I liked the Quaker ideal of never resorting to war. It chimed in well with John Lennon's radical notion of giving peace a chance.

I had ideas about the people I'd meet at the school. The teaching staff would be a quasi-monastic order, wearing dark robes and discussing moral issues. The pupils I imagined as earnest young people who would sit drinking coffee until two in the morning, devising alternative societies and a fairer future for all. The book also explained that Quakers called each other 'friend.' This seemed . . . well . . . friendly. I'd have preferred not to go to school at all. I was convinced I could acquire an excellent education by reading in my room with occasional input from my dad. That didn't seem to be an option, so this school looked as good as any.

My dad could afford to send me there if I won a scholarship, which reduced the fees by twenty per cent. I liked this idea as the scholarship exam was taken in only one subject. I'd avoid being tested on disciplines I didn't get on with like mathematics and science. As I couldn't answer questions on pop music, I accepted it had to be history. One morning in June, I sat alone in the school gym writing essays on fascism, the French Revolution, and the career of Florence Nightingale. Two weeks later, the headmaster asked to see me in his study after assembly. He was standing beside his desk when I arrived. "Congratulations. You've attained the scholarship." He stepped forward. There's no way a man in his fifties can shake hands with a twelve-year-old boy without it being awkward. It was a case of limp meets limper. I didn't see any need to prolong the meeting and turned to go, but he pointed to the chair at the other side of his desk and asked his secretary to bring in two cups of coffee. No teacher had ever offered me coffee before. I took this as acknowledgment of the important step I'd taken towards manhood. People with scholarships drink coffee instead of Coke. He wanted to know what I'd written about in the exam. His field was chemistry and he had no interest in my replies. He speculated on the outcome of the cricket test series between England and the West Indies. I had no idea about sport so couldn't comment. In desperation, he asked where I was going for my summer holiday. The answer was nowhere. You might think my dad was always visiting sites like the Normandy landing beaches or the ruins of concentration camps, but he never travelled. He believed reading about a place was infinitely more effective in understanding it than going there. He also raged against the bad taste of people posing for holiday snaps under the ARBEIT MACHT FREI sign before going back to their luxury hotels.

I wondered why the headmaster was playing for time. I understood when a man arrived brandishing a large camera. The headmaster told me to straighten my tie and smooth back my hair with my fingers. We shook hands again and tried to smile naturally into the camera. It was to be the first time I had my picture in the paper. As soon as the photographer had left, the headmaster waved me towards the door with a brief, "Well done again," glad he didn't have to talk to me anymore.

At the end of the school day, I went home to tell my dad. He looked pleased. As far as I could at such an age, I'd proven myself academically respectable. He knew a good way of celebrating. We walked to Abdul's shop. "He has done well," my dad told Abdul. "He can pick whatever film he wants."

I shrank into myself as Abdul stood in front of me and asked, "What sort of films do you like?" Although I grew to six foot two in my late teens, I was a little boy in those days and Abdul towered above me. Although he was only twenty-two, he came across as very adult in his pressed navy-blue suit over a white shirt. He had close-cropped dark hair, a thin black moustache, and a pot belly inches from my face as I spoke to him.

"I admire the cinematographic innovations in *Citizen Kane*, and I've always found the unreliable narrator device effective in films such as *The Cabinet of Dr Caligari*," I replied.

Abdul sensed I was parroting my dad rather than giving my true opinion, so he tried a different tack. "What's your favourite television programme?"

"*The Goodies.*"

He took a copy of *Monty Python and the Holy Grail* from the shelf. "In that case, you'll love this."

My dad didn't look thrilled with this choice but nodded. "He can also have any snacks he wants."

I picked a large bag of popcorn, a family-size chocolate bar, and a bottle of Coke. My dad and I walked home and sat down to watch the film together. Given his dislike of comedies, it showed how much he wanted to mark the occasion with me. He knew not to expect historical accuracy in a Monty Python film so didn't wince too much at the anachronisms. He chuckled a couple of times and admitted at the end it was a spirited, if silly, piece of storytelling.

It was the last time I celebrated anything to do with that school.

# CHAPTER SIX

SIX WEEKS LATER, I FOUND A LARGE BROWN ENVELOPE addressed to my dad with the school's name in the top left corner. My dad had left it on the hall table. Nearly all the mail was put in a pile to be looked at when he had a moment. He'd never had a moment in twelve years, so wouldn't notice if I opened it. Inside, I found a booklet listing all the behaviours expected from the school's scholars. One of the requirements was 'a good standard of personal hygiene.' This wasn't a problem for me and one area where I differed from my dad. I don't remember him ever smelling bad and his students would have made jokes if they'd noticed anything, but he had no time for male grooming. He showered mainly to wake himself up if he had to go into the university after working all night. He kept a bar of unscented white soap by the shower which he used on his body and hair. He never used the bottles of shower gel and cologne stacked up in the bathroom. The well-meaning aunts who bought me presents also felt compelled to buy him something at Christmas. The books that interested him weren't available in high street shops, and they had no idea what else to buy him, so they fell back on toiletries. It meant I had a steady supply, which I used diligently. From an early age, I've hated my body's natural aromas. It seems as good an argument as any for the non-existence of God. If an all-powerful being created us in his image, why do we smell so bad? Why didn't God give us the scent of roses with a hint of peppermint? To combat this oversight on the almighty's part, I slathered on all the shampoo, shower gel, deodorant, and aftershave my father never used.

The booklet from the school also listed the clothes I needed. It sounded like the outfits for a Victorian gentleman. Day wear was dark trousers, a formal jacket, white shirt, and tie. Evening wear was a suit in navy blue or charcoal grey. I also needed a white t-shirt and shorts for gym as well as a full rugby kit.

My dad looked surprised when I told him about this. When he'd gone to school, he'd taken lessons in grey shorts and sweater. He'd changed for gym by taking his sweater off. He couldn't be bothered questioning it and asked me how much money I needed. I did a quick tot up and gave him a figure. He never used a credit card and disliked writing cheques so kept cash in messy little piles around the house. It would have been a fun treasure hunt for any burglar. He found the money I needed and handed it over. He wouldn't have noticed if I'd doubled the amount. I could have bought all my school clothes and had plenty left over for a couple of new albums. I never did anything like that. My dad distanced himself from day-to-day life in the belief everything would some-how turn out okay. If I needed him to sign something for school, it was no good putting it down next to him. Everything else on the table was always more interesting. I had to place the form in one of his hands and a pen in the other to stand any chance. I took on a lot of household responsibilities from an early age. Neither of us had an interest in keeping the house tidy, but my obsession with personal hygiene extended to having clean clothes. I soon learned how to use the washing machine my mother had bought. It was old, but still did the job. I washed my dad's clothes at the same time. He never queried how clean clothes appeared in his room. Maybe he thought the elves did them. I took money from the piles to buy washing powder, which I considered a legitimate household expense. I never stole from them to buy stuff for myself. My dad's refusal to engage with the mundane world was often infuriating, but there was also something touchingly childlike about it. I wasn't going to take advantage.

It was my first time going into the gentlemen's outfitter on the alleyway leading to the Forum. I felt very grown up as I strode in and announced, "I'm going to need an entire new wardrobe." The shop assistant smirked, so I took the wad of cash out of my pocket and casually thumbed through it. He took me more seriously after that. He measured me without any undue groping and found a suit off the peg that fitted me well. Admiring myself in the mirror, I thought I was quite the dapper man about town. I was also aware of how punchable I'd look to the lads who hung round the alleyway. I changed back into my regular clothes before I went home. I had enough money—my own—to buy a copy of The Doors' *LA Woman* album, which had been released a couple of years too late to be in my mother's collection.

I got dressed up in my new clothes again on Monday morning. I hadn't appreciated how itchy the trousers were. It almost made me yearn for my primary school days of wearing shorts. I covered it all with a big coat, so no one saw how I was dressed, and walked the ten minutes to my new school.

It was divided into four houses. In some schools, a house is little more than a sports club. You play football or cricket for your house in competition with the others. Here, though, the houses were real bricks and mortar places where people ate and slept. I was assigned to the oldest one, which had previously been a Georgian town house belonging to a coffee merchant. As the school had expanded, it had swallowed all the buildings in its path, turning them into science blocks, music rooms, and houses. When I pushed open the glass-panelled front door, the first thing that struck me was the smell. I'd thought a Quaker establishment would have a comforting aroma of oats and chocolate or at least the scents of scholarship—old books, ink, and chalk. During the weekend, the cleaning ladies had gone through the house with industrial strength bleach and the boarders had snacked on oranges and instant noodles. The smell of chlorine was cut through with the bitter tang of pith and the sourness of fake chicken stock.

I'd assumed there'd be a reception desk or at least someone with a clipboard directing the new boys, but no one was there as I went in and looked around. The pupils' parents collectively pumped more than a million pounds a year into the school coffers. It was hard to see where the money was being spent. The walls were bare grey stone. There was nothing on the floor except a worn-down square of coconut matting inside the door. Going straight ahead took me to the kitchen and dining hall where ladies in blue overalls were shouting at each other cheerily as they cleared up after breakfast. As a day boy, I was excused this meal. On the right were two doors with peeling red paint. One led to a games room with a ping pong table in it, the other to a TV room. Old black chairs with yellow stuffing bursting out of them were unevenly lined up in front of a stand with a television and video player.

Turning left, I found a notice board. I saw a typed sheet of paper headed, 'What to do if you are unwell.' Maybe this was my best option. Now I'd had my first sniff of the school, I could persuade some medical professional to confine me to my bed, and I'd come back better prepared in a couple of weeks. The sheet said if I was unwell, I should let Mrs Cairns know. I didn't know how to contact Mrs Cairns any more than I knew how to do anything else. At the top left corner of the notice board was a hand-drawn floorplan of the house and a list of names. By cross-referencing the two, I worked out that three square feet of the building had been allocated to me. I walked along the corridor and opened a green door. I was in a long narrow room, divided into four rows of six desks, each with a wooden bench to sit on and separated from its neighbour by a four-foot-high hardboard partition.

As I entered, twenty-three boys' heads turned to eye me suspiciously, wanting to know who'd let me in. I thought I'd be in the same boat as the others, all of us trying to navigate this strange new environment. Everyone else looked comfortably installed and acted like they'd been friends for years. In time, I'd understand the divisions between them. The scientists despised those who were good at English and history. The sporting types viewed the intellectuals as wimps while the intellectuals considered the sportsmen mindless thugs. Those who liked the guitar-based rock of Bruce Springsteen and Bryan Adams hated the fans of electronica like Soft Cell and Depeche Mode. I didn't know any of that at the time. They all looked united in their resentment of me.

It was one of those times in life where I had missed a vital memo. The booklet I'd read proudly announced, 'We're looking forward to a great new school year starting on Monday 13 September 1982.' I had assumed that was when I needed to show up. I hadn't noticed another letter that had arrived from the school and, naturally, my dad had ignored it. It gave details of the two induction days for new pupils on the Thursday and Friday before the start of term. Everyone else in my year had taken a tour of the school. They'd met the teachers and prefects. Each boy had stood up in front of the others and said three interesting things about himself. Friendships were already forming. They had come to terms with the group as it was and didn't like someone arriving late to change it.

The three square feet I could call my own was my cube. The other boys had already personalised their cubes with photos and posters. Some had pictures of the family or the dog. These were soon taken down as any hint of homesickness was a sign you must be gay. Most boys were keen to trumpet their heterosexuality with glossy shots of women in bikinis cut from magazines. My own cube looked bare and unloved by comparison. I threw my coat over my desk and waited. Nobody spoke to me. I was trying—successfully—not to catch anyone's eye when the other boys left the room. There was no bell or signal I could hear, but at ten to nine, everyone trooped off. In the absence of other instructions, I followed them.

We left the house and went across a parking area into the hexagonal building housing the assembly hall. The five different year groups sat in blocks. The school was dipping its toe in coeducation and had allowed a small number of girls into the two sixth forms. There were twenty of them amongst three hundred boys. I discovered later some of the girls liked these numbers, fancying their odds of finding a boyfriend. On that first day, I felt for them. Every female had lustful eyes boring into her. A lot of the boys had previously been to single sex schools, and this was their first encounter with girls who didn't have staples through their midriffs. The lads were fascinated to see girls did things like scratch their heads and blow their noses. It was almost like they were human.

The sixth side of the hall was the stage, where the headmaster stood, waiting for everyone to sit down. He was a tall, thin man in his early fifties with white hair brushed back from his forehead and square steel-rimmed glasses. On stage with a microphone, he acted more like a compere than a teacher. He welcomed returning pupils back to the school but gave a special shout-out to those joining us for the first time. He talked about all the things that were going to happen during the term, stopping just short of saying, "We've got a great show for you lovely people." He knew the rugby and basketball teams were going to make the school proud. There were exciting guest speakers coming to talk to us. A wildlife expert who'd last been on the radio twenty years ago was hyped up like a visiting head of state. There were to be musical performances, school plays, educational films, no end of high-quality entertainment.

He'd hardly started talking when a realisation hit me like a truck. It made my stomach drop so hard, I had to hang on to the edges of my chair. I was sure I wouldn't be playing for any of the teams. I had no interest in the visiting speakers. The other boys did not look like earnest seekers after Quakerly ideals. A lot of them were big dumb louts. They wouldn't follow me around, hanging on my every word. They'd get bored halfway through the first track of an album and start talking over it. My dad had found this school and filed the matter away as a closed case. There were no alternatives or safety nets. This was not the place for me. I didn't belong here and I was stuck here for the next five years.

# CHAPTER SEVEN

OBITUARIES OF TEACHERS SAY THINGS LIKE, 'He was a committed educator, passionate about helping his students reach their full potential.' They make teaching sound like a vocation. This wasn't true for the staff members at my school. Some were doing their best and/or good at their job but few of them wanted to be there. They fell into two main categories. There were those disappointed by life. Our French teacher, Mr Beaumont, was a good guitarist with a pleasant singing voice. He'd naturally assumed a career in music beckoned and had gone into teaching as a stop-gap to make a bit of money until his big break. After twenty years, his hopes of becoming a pop idol were fading fast. He always found an excuse to bring his guitar into class, ostensibly to teach us the French national anthem or to let us hear songs by Serge Gainsbourg or Johnny Halliday. Really, he wanted an audience. I got on well with him. If I found myself sitting next to him at lunch, we discussed who was the best guitarist The Rolling Stones ever had and if The Beatles could have survived any similar line-up changes. He perked up noticeably during these conversations. Most of the time, his face bore a look of quiet resentment. Life had not given him what he wanted, and he'd never forgive life for that. The English teacher was a man from Cumbria, who saw himself as latter-day lakeside poet. He would slip one of his own odes into poetry appreciation class, hoping we'd be astounded by this undiscovered genius on a par with Wordsworth and Coleridge. When he was found out, he tried to laugh it off as a practical joke but there was so much sadness in his eyes as the pupils mocked his clunky imagery and language that refused to sparkle. After I realised what he was doing, I tried to console him by saying, "There's a line here which isn't too bad." It never seemed to make him feel better.

A larger group of staff members were short, balding men, with bad breath and worse dress sense. Most had the rheumy eyes and wheezy cough of people who drank and smoked too much. These were men who would pass unnoticed in the street and be served last at the pub. In a classroom, however, they had some power. They could make everyone stay late. They could ruin a boy's weekend by putting him on Saturday afternoon detention. Even if they weren't respected, there was a certain wariness of them, which made them feel better about themselves.

An honest obituary of teachers at my school would read, 'He was soured by life and put upon by those who met him, but he enjoyed intimidating small boys.' Their approach to education could be summed up as, "I think you're shit. Now prove me wrong." This might have worked with some of the pupils, who squared their shoulders and were determined to show what they could do. It was a disaster for me. I assumed the teachers knew what they were talking about. If they thought I was shit, that must be what I was. Any confidence I had started draining out of me as soon as I arrived.

The rudest awakening on the first day came in the afternoon when we were told to go to the gym. Mr Wilson, the PE teacher, told us to stand in a straight line. He walked by slowly, looking us up and down. There were two lads from Hong Kong, who could hardly speak English. They were standing close to each other, whispering in nervous Cantonese. Mr Wilson stopped in front of them, "Do you want to hold hands?" They had no idea what he was talking about, so they looked at him, wide-eyed. "Simple question.

Do you want to hold hands?"

One of them took a punt and shook his head.

"Good," said Mr Wilson. "I like people who can make decisions."

Teasing children miles from home in a language they barely understood didn't seem Quakerly. I found out later Mr Wilson had wanted to be an Army sergeant. He'd pictured himself inspecting new recruits, insulting their looks, dress, and anything else he could pick on. After the Army had decided they could live without him, he'd chosen the next best thing and become a PE teacher. He stopped short of saying anything about steers and queers, but looking at a thin boy, said, "We need to be careful with you in the shower. You might slip down the drain." When he reached a fat boy, "We're going to put you in goal. Nothing will get past you. That is, if you can keep your hands off the pies long enough to catch the ball." Coming to me, he said simply, "You have nothing to interest me." Again, not very Quakerly, but I could see his point. Evenings spent lying on my bedroom floor eating chocolate had given me the skinny-boy-with-a-belly body not suited to sporting excellence.

I struggled to see in what ways this was a Quaker school. Even if there was no formal corporal punishment, the teachers were often rough and hurtful. They had no qualms about shoving a boy out of their way or shaking him when he was being slow on the uptake. Most of the pupils showed no interest in embracing Quaker ideals. A lot of them were living away from home for the first time and were scared. Some responded to this by curling in on themselves and saying nothing. Others were loud and obnoxious, shouting crude comments about everything they saw. Racism was rife. Boys from other countries were asked, "Does your father have twelve wives?" or "Is everyone in your country a drug dealer?" The racism wasn't restricted to the pupils. The chemistry teacher casually referred to one of the black lads in his class as Curlylocks. This didn't stand out particularly, as he also had offensive nicknames for the fat boys, the ginger kids, and anyone who wore glasses. The worst was the woodwork teacher, Mr Harmon. He was an old white-haired man who had fought during World War Two and had a deep hatred of all things German. There was a boy in our class called Rainer. Although Rainer was born more than twenty years after the War ended, Mr Harmon acted like Rainer had been a prominent member of the SS. If Rainer fell behind with any task, Mr Harmon would say, "Come on, mein Herr, there's no slave labour to help you now. It'll be your own arbeit that machts you frei." He went off chuckling at his bilingual wit.

Along with the racism, there was sexism. The magazines passed around at the back of the class explained that women—all women, no exceptions—dropped whatever they were doing to have sex with any man who offered. Every boy in the school was convinced all he had to do was go up to a girl and get his wanger out for her to be consumed with lust and submit to his every desire. He was then disappointed by the indifference all the girls showed to both him and his wanger.

The only truly Quakerly thing we had to endure was meeting. If you've never been to a Quaker meeting, it involves sitting in silence for long periods of time. It's the equivalent of a church service, but there are no hymns, Bible readings, or sermons. For thirteen-year-old boys, being forced to sit in silence for forty-five minutes is torture. It wasn't so bad for me as I imagined an album going on to the turntable as the meeting began. All the tracks played in my head. For others, though, it was the longest they'd ever gone without speaking. The urge to stand up and scream, "FUCK!" was hard to resist. The book I'd read about the history of Quakerism talked about how George Fox, the denomination's founder, would sit in silence until he was 'moved of the Lord to speak.' It was an option open to us during meeting, as well. We could share homilies or uplifting anecdotes with the rest of the school if so moved. In reality, most people who spoke in meeting either couldn't bear to keep quiet any longer or wanted to be noticed. A young boy stood up, called out, "To be or not to be, that is the question," and sat down again.

After a pause, one of the older boys stood up. "Surely we can do better than an attention-grabbing cliché."

The first boy stood up again and amended his comment to, "To be or not to be. Is that the question?" He sat down, pleased with his originality.

Meeting was also used as a place for airing grievances. One guy stood up and said, "I'm sixteen. I'm old enough to join the Army and fight for my country, but, in this place, I'm treated like a child and have to be in bed by ten fifteen."

Another boy stood up. "In the Army, lights go out at ten o'clock."

To which another replied, "If you're an officer, you have your own room so you can turn the light out whenever you like."

The first one stood up again. "I'm not saying I want to join the Army. Put it another way, I'm old enough to get married and have kids but I still have to be in bed by ten fifteen."

One of the teachers intervened to point out, "If you have kids, you dream of going to bed at ten fifteen. In fact, you dream of going to bed at all."

The headmaster listened to this with growing despair. If he said anything, it would make meeting more of a debate. Many times, he waited until meeting was over to say, "We can discuss any grievances you may have at *any other time*, but it's not what a Quaker meeting is for."

Each day at school followed the same pattern. The day boys like me arrived after the boarders had finished breakfast. We went to the main hall for assembly or meeting. On the occasions when we weren't sitting in silence, a teacher or pupil had to fill in ten minutes by reading something or talking about a topic they hoped would inspire and uplift. After that, the headmaster would tell us off for whatever we were collectively doing wrong at the time. Once, he gave us the devil for the way we treated the cleaning ladies. I always wished them a cordial good morning and I'd never seen anyone being rude to them. Nevertheless, the headmaster admonished us, "Just because a person may do some scrubbing, it's no reason to call her a scrubber. After all, we could give you lot a name based on something you do." It took a moment to realise our headmaster had called us a bunch of wankers. After he'd finished telling us off, he moved on to the sports results. Despite his optimism at the start of each term, these usually came under the heading of valiant but doomed efforts, "The first fifteen rugby team played well with some new players coming to the fore but, unfortunately, they lost 34 to 8," or "Everyone agreed our basketball team had a good game and the result of 74 to 12 did not reflect how close it was most of the time." After assembly, we had morning lessons, with a fifteen-minute break at eleven o'clock. At one o'clock, we went back to our houses for lunch. This was one of the most painful parts of the day for me. I'd always followed my dad's diet of chocolate and cornflakes. It came as a shock to be confronted by suet dumplings swimming in gravy with occasional lumps of meat and fat. My body refused to ingest any such thing, so I sat there, sipping a glass of water. Fortunately, there was a lengthy break after lunch. In theory, this was the time to play sport. For me, it was time to go home and eat something my body could tolerate. It was this two-hour respite which made the day bearable. My dad was either at the university or absorbed in his books. He also had no idea what the school schedule was, so didn't know whether I was supposed to be at home or not. I grabbed all the biscuits and chocolate I wanted from the kitchen and went upstairs to my bolt hole. Lying on the floor of my bedroom listening to music was my spiritual cleanse. I went home every time the school rules allowed—and many times when they didn't. I could get home in five minutes if I ran. Even the morning break could be a time to run home, listen to one song, and run back, somewhat restored.

It was always a wrench to force myself back into school for afternoon lessons. They were followed by tea, which was no better than lunch. There was a bit more watching of the gates in the evening, so it was harder to slip home. The time between tea and prep was called the hobby hour. It was a chance to learn life skills like car or bike maintenance. We could sing in the school choir or play with the orchestra. The sporting among us worked out in the weights room or played badminton in the gym. A teacher asked me one evening if I'd like to come along for a game of badminton. I found myself using my dad's standard response, "What good would that do?"

I spent hobby hours in the quiet room. This was a converted walk-in larder with a couple of mismatched armchairs and a shelf full of old books. It also had the day's newspapers laid out on a small black walnut table. I should have been learning about world events from the *Times* and the *Guardian*, but I preferred the more sensationalist *Daily Mail*. One evening in July 1983, a couple of headlines caught my eye. 'BAN VIDEO SADISM NOW' and 'Rape of our children's minds.' I settled into one of the armchairs. This sounded like something I definitely wanted to read about.

During the early years of home video, major studios were hesitant about releasing their films in this format, fearing—rightly, as it turned out—that they'd lose control of their product in a world of easy copying and sharing. This left a gap in the market. People wanted something to watch on their new toy. At the same time, video distributors spotted a legal loophole. British film censorship laws applied only to movies shown in a public place. It hadn't occurred to the original lawmakers that films could be watched in private homes. The back pages of video magazines were soon filled with advertisements promising pornographic delights previously seen only in Denmark and Holland. This caused a certain amount of uproar. There's always been a view that the British are too sensitive to see the same explicit material as our American and European cousins. Porn, however, was not the biggest concern. A slew of cheaply made horror films, mostly from Italy and the USA, appeared in video shops. If the tabloids were to be believed, these films did not rely on psychological tension or a slow build-up of dread: they simply splashed blood and entrails all over the screen. In America, they were known as splatter movies. Someone in Britain, either an outraged moralist or a canny marketing executive, called them video nasties.

According to the media storm, an ordinary, decent man had only to see one of these films and he'd roam the streets with a power tool ready to stage a massacre. There was a healthy dose of British snobbery in the panic. A group of MPs was treated to a highlight reel of the grisliest scenes and declared video nasties could deprave and corrupt. Obviously, the MPs themselves weren't depraved or corrupted as they were from well-heeled families and had been to the best schools. They were worried about the effect these films would have on the unwashed working classes. Anyone without the benefit of a private education would be turned into a drooling psychopath.

There was also a lot of talk about protecting children. If video nasties were in homes, it followed kids were watching them. I didn't understand this argument. In most houses, there are things for mummy and daddy which are kept away from the children. Whether it's the car keys or a bottle of Scotch, high shelves and locked cupboards keep grown-up toys away from little hands. Apparently, this wouldn't work with video nasties. Only a total ban could save the young generation.

It didn't take long for Mrs Thatcher to throw her weight behind the campaign. For her, video nasties were a convenient scapegoat. The rioting on Britain's streets during the early 1980s wasn't caused by unemployment or racial discrimination, but by horror films. Get rid of them and we'd all live in peace and harmony.

To convince its readers how deplorable these films were, the Daily Mail described their content in loving detail. Long, enticing accounts concluded with a single word like 'repulsive' or 'disgusting' to show the paper's strong moral compass. If anybody who had seen one of these films was convicted of a crime—even a speeding ticket—the paper howled about how video nasties were turning us all into delinquents. Needless to say, I was fascinated. As these films could magically change someone's entire character, they had the allure of a mind-altering drug. It was said hardened police officers ran out of special screenings and only the strongest could sit through them. I was keen to test my strength.

After the hobby hour came prep, one of the worst parts of the day. The idea was we sat in our cubes and did the work the teachers had set for us. Mr Hamilton, our housemaster, stood down after tea to spend the evening with his wife, so the younger pupils were left under the supervision of older ones. Some of them relished the power and began with a list of threats. "Prep will be extended by five minutes every time there's any noise. Any cheek, it'll be ten minutes. We can stay here until nine o'clock, ten o'clock, or eleven o'clock. It's all the same to me. Any questions?"

"Yes, what about—?"

"That was noise. It earned you an extra five minutes. Anyone else?"

Some of the more rebellious sixth formers refused to go over to the teachers' side. They made it clear they were no different from us and didn't want to work any more than we did. Other seniors were terrified of being put in charge of us, and one of these unwittingly made my life a lot worse.

# CHAPTER EIGHT

FROM DAY ONE, I HAD TROUBLE MAKING FRIENDS. Nothing had changed since primary school. Even more than the kids from other countries, I didn't speak the same language as everyone else. When I remarked one day that the teachers had no popular sovereignty, I wasn't trying to show off. It was the sort of thing I naturally said. It contrasted starkly with the language of the average English public school boy, which consisted of the word 'fucking' repeated endlessly with other words occasionally thrown in. It was used as an intensifier for good or bad. At the lunch table, someone would remark either, "This is fucking delicious," or "This is fucking disgusting." Other times, it meant nothing whatever. The words, "I've got to go to fucking geography now," gave no indication of what the speaker thought about geography. It was part of the boys' everyday speech rhythms. Except when he talked about Mrs Thatcher, my dad didn't use language like this, so it was a shock to hear it so often. It wasn't the sort of talk I expected to hear from Quakers. In an attempt to fit in, I tried using it, but it didn't sound right in my voice.

I had hoped to bond with people through my musical knowledge. It was cool to know about pop music, wasn't it? Unfortunately, mine was the wrong kind. Music was everywhere in the school. Conflicting tunes blared out of every study, dormitory, and cube room. Among those who liked pop, Madonna was the undisputed queen. When I asked people what they liked about her, the response was usually, "She's so horny," rather than anything about her musical talents. I tried listening to her and didn't hear anything which hadn't been done with more personality and attitude by Debbie Harry and Chrissie Hynde. I made the mistake of sharing this view and the boys exchanged knowing glances.

Hip hop was still in its infancy, but a small group had already latched on to Afrika Bambaataa's 'Planet Rock' and Grandmaster Flash's 'The Message.' A couple of years later, Run DMC and LL Cool J gave them more to choose from.

They didn't share my tastes. The Beatles were classed alongside Beethoven as something their parents listened to. I didn't see any reason to hide who I was and put up pictures of The Beatles and The Doors in my cube.

One day, a boy sidled up to me. "I like The Beatles too," he murmured, conspiratorially, like he was doing a drug deal. It was enough for us to form a friendship. Andrew was tall and gangly with greasy hair and spots. He wouldn't have been most people's first-choice friend. I was also shocked by how little he knew of The Beatles for someone who claimed to be a fan. He thought 'Strawberry Fields Forever' was on *Sergeant Pepper*, and once asked me if *A Hard Day's Night* and *Help!* were two different names for the same film. Despite his shortcomings, it was good to have a friend. I had someone to sit next to in class and at lunch. During the many times every day when we waited around for something to happen, I had someone to wait with. I took these opportunities to educate Andrew, not only about The Beatles, but about music in general. He listened, but didn't take much in. He never did well in the snap tests I gave him.

Then a couple of things happened.

My whole year was called into the school hall for a meeting with the headmaster. He began, "I want to speak to you today about sex . . ." Immediately, we sat up straighter. This promised to be more interesting than his talks about exam procedures. He continued, ". . . drugs, drinking, smoking, and theft." We were now fully engaged. This sounded like a talk that would make a pretty good movie. Unfortunately, it went downhill from there, because his advice on all of them was like a video nasty title, "Don't." I was intrigued by his caveats, though. "Don't have sex, but if you must, use contraception. Don't take drugs, but if you must, stick to cannabis rather than heroin or cocaine. Don't drink, but if you must, have beer or cider instead of spirits." I was waiting for him to say, "Don't steal, but if you must, wear gloves so there are no prints left at the scene."

The headmaster was clearly embarrassed about mentioning gay sex but had no choice. Rumours were circulating about a new disease. He told us firmly, "You may have girlfriends, but you may not have sexual intercourse with them, and you are also not permitted to have sex with each other, but if you must, it seems protection is now as important in the homosexual world as in the heterosexual. Statistically, five people in this room will discover they're homosexual." Glances darted round the room, looking for the five most likely. Forty pairs of eyes bore into me. Suspicions had been mounting for some time. The first piece of evidence against me was the way I smelled. After shave was colloquially known as 'poof juice.' My copious use of shower gel, deodorant, and cologne made me smell, as one boy put it, "like a tart's handbag." The other was my lack of enthusiasm for Madonna. It had nothing to do with my finding her music derivative. If I didn't like such a sexy woman, it was probably because I was gay. I could have pointed out Madonna's status as a gay icon, but proving myself an expert in matters homosexual wouldn't have helped my cause.

I want to make it clear I didn't see anything wrong with being gay. I'd read about Oscar Wilde and Joe Orton, and quite fancied life as a gay playwright, even though it didn't end well for either of them. The truth is, I didn't know what I was. Me having sex with *anyone*—male or female—was like me walking on the moon. It would be interesting but so unlikely it wasn't worth thinking about.

To be fair to the headmaster, he concluded his talk by saying, "If someone you know thinks he might be homosexual, give him all the support you can. He's going to be anxious and confused. He'll need his friends to stick by him."

Many of the lads sat back and folded their arms with a look that said, "If my friend turns out to be gay, I'll never speak to him again."

The same evening, I did something that removed all doubt from the other boys' minds.

Julia was the girl who most dreaded taking us for prep. She was quiet and shy, the type who liked to sit under a tree with a good book. She reminded me of me. All she wanted was a bolt hole where she could be alone. I'd have liked to get to know her, but sixth form girls never fraternised with junior boys. She was an object of lust to many as she had long curly brown hair and hazel eyes, a short, curvy body, with large breasts. She often exploited her air of vulnerability to persuade one of the sixth form boys to take prep in her place. It didn't work every time, though. On this fateful evening, we were sitting in the cube room, watching the door to see who our prefect for the evening would be. Julia came in, trying to look resolute, but the boys saw the fear in her eyes. "Right, sit down everyone, please," she said in her soft, breathy voice. Her first mistake was to say "please." It was a sign of weakness. I slumped on my bench. I hated preps like this. I've never been a big fan of authority, but the only thing I like disturbing my quiet is music. Even if I didn't want to do any work, I needed a certain level of peace in order to read the *Melody Maker*. There was also a danger, if we made too much noise, it would reach Mr Hamilton, who lived in an annexe off the main house. If his home evenings were disturbed, he stormed in, distributing detentions to the guilty and innocent alike. Detention on Wednesday or Saturday afternoon didn't worry the other lads much. They were either stuck in the detention room or stuck in some other room, so it wasn't a strong deterrent. For me, these afternoons were prime music-listening time, and I resented any disruption of them. The cube room slowly descended into chaos. One boy shouted to his friend across two banks of desks. They continued their high-volume conversation despite Julia's suggestion that they wait until after prep. One boy had a bottle of ginger ale and was not prepared to share one drop of it with his peers. He was ready to fight to the death in defence of it and used the bottle as a club to take down anyone who came near. Another had a tennis ball and set up an impromptu cricket match, with a physics textbook as the bat.

Julia was becoming increasingly agitated. Mr Hamilton had been known to put the prefect on detention for not keeping better control and Julia liked to stay out of trouble. She told us if we weren't quiet, she'd get angry. Some people are scary when they get angry; others are not. Everyone ignored her. She threatened to extend prep by ten minutes, but she knew if we all walked out, there wasn't much she could do to stop us. She stamped her feet. The guys stamped theirs in response. It sounded like the opening of 'We Will Rock You.' She was on the point of tears but knew it would be fatal. Finally, when there was a brief lull in the noise, she said, "If no one makes a sound for the rest of prep . . ." She paused, gulped, and added in a rush, "I'll show you my boobs." The boys looked at each other, trying to work out if she was bluffing, then went to their cubes and started working in silence. Julia initially looked relieved. She had achieved her goal of bringing order to the room, but at what cost? As the minutes ticked towards nine o'clock and all remained quiet, I guessed what she was thinking. She'd assumed her promise would keep everyone quiet for a few minutes, but they wouldn't be able to resist talking for long. She didn't know boys of thirteen and fourteen would endure any hardship or deprivation for the slightest chance of seeing a pair of breasts on a real live girl. She was like a politician who promises untold riches to the people, safe in the knowledge he'll never be elected. When the clock outside the cube room chimed, she realised she'd have to make good on her manifesto. The boys stood up and advanced on her like lions on a wounded gazelle. I looked into Julia's face. I was hoping to see some roguish delight in her eyes, part of her relishing the prospect of doing something naughty and outrageous. All I saw was the same sad resignation of someone who hates going to the dentist but does it anyway. She started plucking at different parts of her blouse, not sure whether to unbutton it or pull it up from the bottom hem. A tear ran down her cheek.

I stood up, made my way through the crowd, took Julia by the arm, and led her out of the room. I moved quickly and surprised everyone. By the time they knew what was happening, we were already out the door. Julia and I went along the hall to the corridor where the sixth formers had their studies. She detached herself from me before anyone saw us together, muttered, "Thanks," and disappeared into her study. I knew it wouldn't be a good idea to go back to the cube room. Even though it was a cold evening, I went home without my jacket.

I thought about being ill for the rest of the week. I was scared about going in the next day, but also intrigued to see what the reaction would be. If Julia had told her friends what had happened, I might be a feminist icon. All was quiet as I walked into the cube room. I half-expected my cube to be trashed, but the only thing I noticed was my jacket was in a slightly different position. I picked it up tentatively and shook it, in case it contained a live rat. I didn't see anything amiss, so I put it on, and went to my first lesson. The morning went normally. There were a few giggles behind me, but nobody said anything. At the end of the history lesson, the teacher beckoned me over. "Showing solidarity with one of history's oppressed minorities?" he asked me.

"What do you mean?"

"Look at the back of your jacket."

I took it off. A pink cloth triangle from someone's wash flannel had been sewn onto the back of my jacket. I do mean sewn. It wasn't stuck on with glue. Someone had taken a lot of trouble to stitch it into place. The history teacher handed me a small pair of scissors. I sat down and removed the triangle without damaging the jacket.

In the minds of my fellows, all doubts about my sexuality had vanished. It had nothing to do with rescuing a girl from a vulnerable situation. If I didn't want to see a pair of tits, I must be gay. It was that simple.

The 1980s were a different time. Gay bookshops were routinely raided by the Obscene Publications Squad. The book, *Jenny Lives with Eric and Martin*, was accused of perverting the innocent for daring to suggest a young girl raised by two gay men might be happy and healthy. Churchmen promised homosexuality would bring down God's wrath, not only on those who practised it, but on people who defended or supported it. Mrs Thatcher's attitude was ambivalent. In 1967, she was one of the few Conservative MPs who voted to legalize sex between two men over twenty-one in a private place. She also made a speech including the infamous line, "Children who need to be taught to respect traditional moral values are being taught that they have an inalienable right to be gay." Her approach was: let the gay men we already have do what they want, but let's not make any more of them.

Being confirmed as the gayest of the gay didn't bother me much in itself. It might have been true: I didn't know back then. It impacted my life in the school. Any boy who spent time with me was assumed to be my lover, so no one talked to me. There wasn't a dramatic moment when Andrew announced he wasn't my friend anymore. He started standing apart from me. Arriving in the dining hall, I found he was already seated with someone on either side of him. It was a blow. I felt more obviously like an outcast, but life was still bearable, because I had my bolt hole. I spent as much time as possible at home. If I ran into my dad while foraging in the kitchen, form required he ask how my day was going. He then told me about whatever historical conundrum was occupying him at the time. When he got bored and wanted to go back to his books, I returned to my room. It was my space with my TV, my record player, my headphones, and my albums. Whatever happened at school, it couldn't touch me there.

# CHAPTER NINE

THE SCHOOL DAY STARTED AT TEN TO NINE. I set my alarm for ten past eight. If I got a spurt on, I could be up and showered in twenty minutes. No matter how pressed for time I was, I never skimped on my ablutions. I dressed in ten minutes. It took me another ten to walk to school. The problem was, if I'd been listening to music until three in the morning, the last thing I wanted to do when the alarm went off was get a spurt on. Normally, it didn't matter. There was no roll call taken at assembly. I could sneak in through a side gate and mingle with the others as they came out of assembly. I was present and correct in the first class and no one was any the wiser. One Wednesday morning, I walked into the school a minute before nine o'clock. The one trouble with the side gate was that the high hedges growing on either side of it stopped me checking if the coast was clear before I walked in. Once I went through the gate, I was out in the open with no chance of backing out. Seeing Mr Wilson the PE teacher approaching, I sighed. "What are you doing strolling in at this time?" he demanded in his parade ground bark.

It wasn't the tone but his choice of words which annoyed me so much. "Why did you say strolling?" I snapped back. He didn't have an answer, so I continued, "What is it about the way I'm walking that suggests strolling?"

"You'd better tell Mr Hamilton you were late before I do."

"Yeah," I responded, dully.

"Yes, sir," he corrected me.

I resisted the urge to tell him 'sir' was reserved for officers, something he'd never be. Instead, I said, "Yes, friend." He bridled, and I pointed out, "This is a Quaker school. It's what Quakers call each other. You can't argue with that."

I walked away, thinking I'd heard the last of it. I was surprised to be pulled out of French class and told to go to the headmaster's study. He was sitting behind his desk, looking severe. Mr Wilson was sitting in front of the desk, looking like a man determined to be strong in the face of all the wrongs done to him. The headmaster pointed me to the seat next to Mr Wilson. "I think an apology is in order, don't you?"

"I agree." I turned to Mr Wilson expectantly.

"No, *you* to apologize to *him.*"

I raised my eyebrows. "For what, exactly?"

"He says you were rude to him."

"I called him friend. Is it wrong to speak to someone as a Quaker in a Quaker school?"

"Well . . ."

The headmaster was wrong-footed so I pressed home my advantage. "I think Mr Wilson will be the first to admit he used emotive language."

The headmaster gave Mr Wilson an enquiring look. Mr Wilson's face was reddening. A thrill ran through me as I realised he had no idea what emotive language was. "Well . . . I . . . what I said was . . ." he stammered.

The headmaster jumped in to save him. "You will report to Mr Wilson after lunch this afternoon."

"To what end?" I wanted to know.

"That's for Mr Wilson to decide."

"I don't think you've thought this through, headmaster." I didn't mind calling him this. It was a simple fact he was the headmaster, so the word didn't imply any respect. "You're falling back on the stock teacher's response of putting the pupil on detention. The situation is more complex and warrants a more nuanced approach."

For a moment, he looked like he was going to engage with me seriously, but he took the easy way out. "I've made my decision." He waved me away. I left the room, disappointed in him. This was also a bitter blow. There were no lessons after lunch on Wednesday and I had plans. I was dipping my toe into progressive rock at the time and wanted to play albums by The Moody Blues and Pink Floyd back-to-back to see which I liked best. This was so much more appealing than an afternoon with Mr Wilson that I thought about not showing up and taking the consequences. Something told me this would be pushing my luck too far. At two o'clock, I pulled open the double doors leading into the gym and saw Mr Wilson. He was standing with his legs apart and his hands on his hips, trying to look like Superman. Worse was the look of delight on his face. My ass was his for the next hour and he was going to enjoy every minute of it.

I had no idea what a detention in a gym would be like. I thought he might make me run up and down until I threw up or passed out. "You're going to learn some important lessons this afternoon." Hearing that, I despised him even more. It would have been better if he'd admitted he enjoyed it without pretending it was for my benefit.

He presented me with a net full of twenty dirty footballs and told me to clean them. He directed me to the block of four toilets attached to the gym. He didn't give me any cloth or brush. He wanted me to get my hands dirty, washing them at the basin. I always did everything possible to avoid dirty hands and came up with a different way. If I dropped a football into a toilet bowl and pulled the chain, the water from the flush cleaned the ball nicely. I had them all as new in five minutes. I didn't want to let on I'd finished so quickly, so I sat on one of the toilets for a while. In the years before mobile phones, there wasn't much to do at times like these. I hadn't brought a book or a copy of the *New Musical Express*, so I sat there and played a couple of songs in my head.

I went back to his little room, where he was working at his desk. I couldn't imagine what he was writing. What class notes does a gym teacher have to write? 'Made some boys run around for a while. It was pointless.' I showed him the bag full of balls. If he'd achieved his ambition of becoming an Army sergeant, he'd have had a pair of white gloves to run over them. As it was, he reluctantly grunted his approval of the job I'd done and handed me his boots. They were caked with mud. I was tempted to drop those down the toilet as well, but I took them outside and used a stick to scrape most of the mud from around the studs. I polished them on a patch of wet grass.

He smirked. "You've just cleaned my boots. I bet you wish you'd called me sir now." I didn't say anything. He took my silence as proof I was suitably cowed. "You're feeling pretty emotive now, aren't you? All right, you can go."

I walked away, duly chastened and determined to live a better life in future. Or, to put it another way, I was burning with vengeful fury.

# CHAPTER TEN

YOU'VE NO DOUBT GUESSED BY NOW Mr Wilson was the sort of person who owned a red sports car. It was his pride and joy. I'd seen footage of the riots in Brixton and Toxteth on the news and was impressed by how brightly cars burned on being hit by a Molotov cocktail. My dad had a petrol-driven lawnmower. He hadn't been into our garden for more than ten years. I liked the way he'd let it grow into a wilderness where squirrels roamed with foxes roaming after them. The cobweb-covered lawnmower stood in the garage with a nearly full can of petrol beside it. It was simple enough to make a Molotov cocktail. Fill a milk bottle with petrol. Soak a length of cotton wool in petrol. Put the cotton wool in the mouth of the bottle to make a fuse. Light. Throw at target. One of these landing on Mr Wilson's car would cause a nice surface blaze across the roof. With luck, the conflagration would find its way to the petrol tank and the whole vehicle would go up. The thing about petrol, though, is that it smells. I couldn't shake the idea that, however careful I was, I'd spill some on my hands or clothes. I had this image of the headmaster lining up the whole school and subjecting us to a sniff test. I didn't want to be found out, not because I feared being expelled, but because I wanted to prove I was clever enough to get away with it. I needed something a bit less odorous.

I don't know where I got this from—a conversation round the lunch table or something on TV—but I'd heard a potato jammed into the exhaust pipe would stop a car from going. I liked this idea. For someone like Mr Wilson, his car not working would hit him like impotence. Our larder at home was a graveyard for vegetables. My dad occasionally bought them when he had some idea of eating more healthily. He never followed through by cooking them, though, so they rotted and sprouted on the larder floor.

I waited three weeks. On Monday mornings, the first lesson after break was biology. The science block was next to the gym. Mr Wilson always parked his car between the two buildings. My plan was simple. I would head towards the science block with a potato secreted in my pocket. When I reached the back of his car, I'd crouch to tie my shoelace and push the potato into the exhaust pipe before joining my fellows. No one would suspect a thing.

On the chosen day, I had the potato hidden behind a pile of music magazines on my desk in the cube room. It was an old potato which smelled a little. It's the one time I was grateful for the chlorinated cleaning product pervading the house. I spent break time flipping through one of the magazines. As I put it back on the pile, I took the potato and slipped it into my pocket. Nobody was paying any attention to me. At the end of break, I picked up my biology book and followed the others out. Everything was going according to plan until I knelt down behind the car. I was almost at eye level with the exhaust pipe and realised I'd misjudged the size. The pipe was a lot narrower than I'd expected, and the potato was too thick. I thought the pipe might act as a corer so I could leave the middle of the potato inside while taking away the hollow outer part. I tried this, pushing as hard as I could, but the opening of the pipe wasn't sharp enough to cut into the potato. I couldn't stay there for longer than it took to tie my shoelaces. I walked away. Many people would have abandoned the whole idea. My mind was working quickly at finding an alternative solution. I needed something softer than a potato for the exhaust pipe to bore a hole into. In an anteroom to the house kitchen, loaves of sliced bread, tubs of margarine, and industrial-sized jars of flavourless jam were laid out so the pupils could have a snack at break time. They were always cleared away before lunch but would still be there if I hurried. I went back to the house. All the dinner ladies were hard at work in the kitchen. No one saw me as I found a packet of white bread and carried it outside as casually as possible. I was thinking on my feet and hadn't considered how incriminating it would be if anyone saw me. I hid the packet as best I could behind my biology textbook. Everyone else was in class. I looked up at the science lab windows but didn't see any suspicious faces peering out. I squatted behind the car again. Opening the packet, I pushed the exhaust pipe into the middle of the loaf. It worked well. Pulling the loaf back, I saw a dirty hole had been drilled through the centre. The exhaust pipe was stuffed full of bread. I pushed it in a bit further so it was less obvious. A few crumbs lingered on the outside of the pipe, but I brushed those away. I stood up and turned slowly through three hundred and sixty degrees. I was unobserved. Going back to the house, I dumped the incriminating loaf into the bin under the empty bread packets. I'd have aroused too much suspicion if I'd gone to biology class so late, so I secreted myself in the toilet and came out in time to join the others on their way to the next lesson.

As I sat in sociology class, I had some insight into how a murderer must feel. I played the scene in my head over and over to see if I'd left any clues. Had I done something stupid like drop a handkerchief with my name tag on it at the crime scene? Had I left fingerprints on the exhaust pipe? I didn't know what the school's capacity for forensic investigation was, but maybe the science teachers would work out something between them.

The next morning, I went into the school assembly hall and sat down. There were no inspirational readings or music recitals. The headmaster stood up and took the microphone. "Yesterday evening," he began, "a member of our staff drove home, unaware anything was awry." He was theatrical but stern like he was doing the commentary on a true crime programme. "Before long, though, he realised something was seriously wrong. He was having trouble breathing and began to cough as the inside of his car filled with fumes. He made an emergency stop on the motorway. The authorities were alerted and he was taken to hospital where he was treated for smoke inhalation. Fortunately, he was discharged later and was able to sleep in his own bed. It's a miracle nobody was killed or seriously injured."

I stopped myself from sitting up and taking too obvious an interest. All this talk about emergency stops and smoke inhalation came as a surprise. My understanding had been, if the exhaust pipe was blocked, the car wouldn't start. I felt a twinge of guilt. I'd wanted to inconvenience and embarrass Mr Wilson, but not endanger his life. I certainly hadn't wanted to put anyone else at risk. Suddenly, it was all more serious than an exercise in what I could get away with.

"Investigations were made and the cause was found to be an act of mindless vandalism," continued the headmaster. I objected to him calling it mindless. It was first a carefully planned and then a brilliantly improvised act of vandalism.

"I know who did it." He looked round the room dramatically. "Oh yes, I know. I want to give the person responsible the chance to own up."

Everyone looked around to see if the guilty party would crack. I did too, for form's sake, but I couldn't believe the headmaster was trying such a lame psychological stunt. If he'd really known, he wouldn't have been talking about it in assembly. I'd have been in his study, and he'd have been making futile attempts to contact my dad.

After five minutes of silence, no one had broken down and confessed. The headmaster announced he would speak to every single person in the school during the day. I'd noticed something about the headmaster's description of the incident: the lack of several important details. He hadn't said which member of staff was affected or what the act of vandalism involved. It was like something out of an old-fashioned detective novel:

"I didn't murder his lordship. I never even touched the candlestick."

"How did you know his lordship was killed with the candlestick?"

"You said!"

"Oh no, sir, I didn't mention the candlestick and I never said the victim was his lordship. So once again, I must ask how you knew."

Was the headmaster really hoping someone would come into his study and say, "I didn't put the bread anywhere near Mr Wilson's car"?

The atmosphere as we queued up outside the headmaster's study was light-hearted. Nobody looked worried about being falsely accused and it made a change from being in lessons. I spent the waiting time thinking about what expression to assume. I didn't want any hint of triumph or fear in my face. I settled for looking bored but resigned, as if all this was a waste of my time, but I understood why the headmaster had to do it.

When my turn came, I walked into his study and he told me to close the door. As I sat down, I was surprised to see him grinning in a conspiratorial way. "I know I shouldn't be saying this, but there are times he annoys the hell out of me, as well."

Just for a second, it almost worked. He knew it was me and he understood why I'd done it. He might even have done the same thing. He'd have to exact a punishment because, hey, it was his job, but first we'd have a man-to-man chat about how irritating Mr Wilson was.

It *almost* worked. I realised just in time he'd used these same words to everyone who'd passed through his study. I appreciated the way he'd upped his game since assembly. This was a more sophisticated way of drawing out a confession. I adopted what I hoped was a look of mild confusion. "I'm not sure I follow you, headmaster."

He tried an approach better adapted to me. "I know you and Mr Wilson have had your differences."

This was the moment where I felt real fear. I'd been hoping the fierce rush of school life over the last three weeks had made everyone forget about our differences. I raised my eyebrows like this was interesting news. "I didn't know we were talking about Mr Wilson."

"Maybe we are and maybe we're not, but if we were talking about Mr Wilson, would you happen to know anything about it?"

"Are you saying something was done to Mr Wilson's car?" I asked, frowning as I tried to make sense of what he was saying.

"Was something done to Mr Wilson's car?" he asked.

I spread my hands. "Obviously I don't know what happened, but I have no residual ill will towards Mr Wilson. I was out of line, and he did what he had to do. I learned a lesson and moved on. I can't say I've dwelt on the matter." I found myself admiring this mature version of myself and wished I could be more like him.

"Okay, thank you." The headmaster nodded to the door.

I stopped myself punching the air as I walked out. He'd interrogated me and I'd revealed nothing but name, rank, and serial number. The euphoria was short-lived. Can revenge be truly satisfying if the other person doesn't know who's taken it? I wanted Mr Wilson to realise he'd underestimated me. I couldn't see any way of making him know.

# CHAPTER ELEVEN

I T WAS MADE CLEAR SPORT WAS compulsory and unpleasant things would happen to people who didn't show up. I worked out how to play the system by using mathematics so simple anyone except a PE teacher could understand it. A football match lasts ninety minutes. If I didn't go, the worst fate which befell me was an hour-long detention. That left me thirty minutes to the good. The figures were even more in my favour during the summer. Cricket matches are interminable. The most important ones go on for several days. Even the limited over games we played at school lasted four hours. On average, I missed three matches before anyone noticed. Detention was supposed to be an effective deterrent, but I'd always take an hour picking up litter over twelve hours playing cricket. After a while, I stopped going to detentions as well. The booklet I'd read before starting at the school warned, 'If you miss, or are late for, detention, you'll be in for serious trouble.' It was never explained what this trouble was. What could the teachers do? I'm not advocating a return to the days of corporal punishment, but it might have been effective at keeping me in check. As it was, if I missed detention, I was put on another—usually longer—one. If I didn't go to that, the only threat they had left was telling my dad. As he never looked at his mail, picked up the phone, or answered the doorbell, it wasn't a threat which could be carried out. I felt fireproof.

My sense of invulnerability increased after I became part of the school's marketing strategy.

The late-night slot on BBC2 was regularly given over to academics, journalists, and politicians debating issues through a fog of pipe smoke. My dad and I sometimes watched these programmes, especially if the topic was history. Historians loved to prove each other wrong and could barely contain their glee as they said, "Dr Aylmer seems to have forgotten an important piece of evidence," or "Surely I don't need to remind you of the work done on this issue by E. H. Lewis." On the occasions when discussion turned to the Holocaust, though, there was a distinct shift in tone. Occasionally, someone suggested there weren't as many as six million Jewish people in the countries under Nazi control. Another might question whether the architecture of Auschwitz allowed it to be as efficient a killing machine as generally understood. The responses to these comments were along the lines of, "He's made a pact with the Devil," or "He's clearly motivated by a vicious anti-Semitism." Point, counterpoint, arguing, and disagreeing were all part of the intellectual cut and thrust—except on this particular topic. In any other area of historical debate, an unpopular view could lead to charges of intellectual laziness or lacking academic rigour. Any deviation from the accepted view on the Holocaust was different. It was *morally* reprehensible. More to sort this out in my own mind than anything else, I wrote a short essay called, 'Is history ready for the Holocaust?' I argued the wounds inflicted on the world by the Nazis were still too raw to allow of normal historical discourse. All we could do for the moment was work to ensure nothing like this ever happened again. Only when all the people directly or indirectly affected were dead would we have sufficient distance to treat it in the same way as any other part of history. I showed the essay to my dad, who declared it to be, "A succinct encapsulation of an interesting idea." This was high praise, coming from him, and I went back to my bedroom feeling happy with myself. My dad was a regular contributor to a magazine called *History Now* and occasionally met with the editor over lunch to discuss future articles. At one of these meetings, my dad showed the editor my essay. The second page of *History Now* printed a short, provocative piece, designed to spark lively arguments among readers. The editor wanted to feature my essay in this spot. My dad agreed without consulting me and told me about it after he arrived back from his lunch. My only question was, "How much do I get?" I hoped I'd be paid at least the price of a few new records. My dad told me sternly that publishing in academic journals wasn't about money but about building a reputation.

The piece was printed and attracted the hoped-for comments. Some agreed we needed to give the topic more time. Others said anything that happened five minutes ago was now history and could be subjected to the same analysis as an event from Roman times or the Middle Ages. Nobody accused me of making a pact with the Devil. Shortly after, the headmaster announced in morning assembly he'd like to share something with us. He proceeded to read my essay. At the end, he asked me to stand up in case my schoolmates had forgotten what I looked like.

It did nothing for my peer group rating. I didn't think there was anything inherently homosexual about writing articles for history magazines, but it was one more reason why I must be gay. It did, however, increase my standing with the school authorities. The next issue of the school prospectus carried a small photo of me on the seventh page along with a puff piece about my achievement. It was thanks to the school's advanced teaching methods that pupils were publishing in well-known academic journals at such an early age. I resented the school taking credit, but I saw I could use it to my advantage. I figured it would be embarrassing for the school to throw me out now they were using me as a poster boy. I started arriving later, leaving earlier, and missing lessons. Often, I didn't go in at all for a couple of days. If anyone asked me about it, I muttered something about being unwell.

I had found the secret to surviving school: spend as little time in it as possible. Then something happened.

One evening as my dad was pouring cornflakes into a bowl for his supper, he muttered to himself disconsolately. I asked what was bothering him. "Thatcher," he replied. I smiled, assuming he was going to start one of his rants about everything that was wrong with her. "It turns out historians do not have a huge role to play in her economic revolution."

"Is that a surprise?" I asked.

"No," he admitted, "but what is a surprise is how quickly she's putting a torch to everything good about this country." He paused and sighed. "Pearce had a meeting with the Vice-Chancellor today. The Vice-Chancellor said he supports the history department a hundred per cent, but budget restrictions might force his hand."

"Meaning?" I asked.

"Meaning we might be closed down."

I went to bed feeling vaguely uneasy, but not too worried. My dad was well-respected. Even if this department closed, I was confident he'd find a job easily enough at another university. I even dared to hope that, if we moved, it would be my ticket to another school where I could start again.

I didn't hear any more about it for a month and assumed it had been a false alarm. My dad called me into the living room. I sat down at the table where he worked and felt a stab of fear as he rolled a cigarette. What did he want to discuss with me at length? "I've been looking round for another job, but it's the same all over the country. So . . . . I've cast my net further afield." I thought he might be talking about one of the great European universities. I liked the idea of living in Paris or Heidelberg. "I've been offered a position at Miami University."

"Are you sure you want to be in America?" I asked. "I doubt if historians play a huge part in Ronald Reagan's revolution, either."

He smiled. "True, but it appears to be the only option for the present."

Spending all night and most of the day in my bedroom had left me paper white. I had a feeling the Miami sun would reduce me to a pile of ashes. "I can't see myself heading down to the beach with my surfboard."

He shook his head. "You would think Miami University is in Florida, but it's actually in Ohio."

I had no picture of Ohio in my head, but I shrugged and paraphrased a famous song. "I might like to be in America."

He didn't pick up on the reference and said slowly, "Yes, you might, but not yet. There's a three-month probation period. I don't want to uproot you if it doesn't work out."

I didn't tell him how much I wanted to be uprooted, so said vaguely, "I'm sure it'll be fine, whatever happens."

"I don't know what accommodation will be available over there. It's better if I go out alone, at least at the beginning."

My dad didn't want me to come with him, but I was used to being by myself most of the time. I didn't think my life would change much, even with my father four thousand miles away instead of downstairs. "I'll look after this place for you."

"There are always expenses when you relocate. I've decided to let this place out. I've spoken to Mr Hamilton. He's agreed you can board from the start of next term."

He picked up the paper he was working on, signifying the discussion was over. I went to my room and slumped down on the bed. I looked round my cosy bolt hole and knew it would soon be taken away. I could take one or two books, and some music papers, but I couldn't take my record player. Any records would be scratched to pieces in the rough and tumble of a dormitory. My dad knew how much I disliked the school. Or did he? Any time he asked me how school was going, I said, "All right." This was my reward for not speaking up.

Even so, I felt betrayed. I'd seen myself as my dad's pet hamster. It turned out I was more like his goldfish and was flushed down the toilet when he had no more use for me.

# CHAPTER TWELVE

In my time as a day boy, I'd never set foot in the dormitories. There hadn't been any reason to go upstairs in the house. Now I was expected to sleep in a long, narrow room which smelled of socks, cheap deodorant, and sheets which were only changed after someone lodged a complaint. I was assigned the one empty bed in the place. I had six by three feet of bed plus two square feet of locker. My first thought on seeing the space was, "This is not my bolt hole."

As I was gazing glumly at my bed, Jason came in. He was one of those boys you met sometimes in expensive schools. There's no way he could have passed the entrance exam, but his daddy was rich, and he was a big strong lad who played in all the teams. He groaned loudly as he saw me moving in. "Oh no! You're not sleeping next to me, are you? You come anywhere near me in the night and I'll smack your head in."

I wasn't feeling defiant but gave him the best pout I could muster. "Even if I were gay, I'd be out of your league."

It took him a moment to process this. "You're finally owning up to being gay," he said, missing the point. "Keep the fuck away from me."

I didn't sleep that night. A boarding school dormitory is never silent. The evening's masturbation was completed with admirable efficiency, but the gurgling and farting went on all night. In the light of day, I could dismiss Jason's words as mere posturing. In a dark room, everything was more threatening. Jason had said any move on his part would be purely defensive, but I couldn't rule out a pre-emptive first strike. I curled myself into a ball with some idea of being a smaller target.

This wasn't the worst aspect of boarding school life. Next to the dormitory was a bathroom area with a row of basins along one wall and toilet cubicles opposite. The boys competed to see who could generate the most noise and the worst smells. The idea of these people knowing I ever went to the toilet was appalling. I wondered if I could be prescribed some pills that would stop me needing to go until the end of term.

There was also the question of washing. The only showers were in a communal area with no cubicles or even partitions down in the basement. They were switched on for an hour before breakfast and after sports in the afternoon. There was no way I was going to shower with anyone else. My words were what I made public, even if they weren't always appreciated. My body was the private me, something to be hidden. The spots on my back and the places sprouting hair for no good reason played no part in the way I presented myself to the world. On the other hand, I couldn't bear not washing. As much as I hated anyone seeing my body, people smelling it was a whole lot worse. On the first morning, I covered myself in the deodorant and cologne I'd brought from home, but it wasn't a long-term solution.

By two o'clock on the second night, everyone else in the dormitory was snoring. I still couldn't sleep so got out of bed and went for a wander round the house. None of the internal doors were locked so I roamed freely. I had no desire to go into any of the other dormitories and watch people sleep. I ended up in the television room. I never went there during the day, as it was usually a war zone. Unless there was a James Bond film on, which everyone wanted to see, different factions fought over what to watch. In the middle of the night, though, the room was pleasantly quiet. Unfortunately, British channels hadn't embraced the idea of twenty-four-hour TV in those days and there was nothing on. The video player on the stand next to the TV gave me an idea. I could rent a couple of videos from Abdul and spend the night watching those instead of being curled up sleeplessly in bed.

The next day, I left the school grounds and went for a walk. I had lost my bolt hole, but still spent as little time in the school as I could. I often walked past our house—except it didn't look like our house anymore. A car was parked outside which didn't belong there. Someone had put coloured plastic in the window of my room— yes, mine!—to create a stained-glass effect. It wasn't something I would ever put in my room, and I resented it. Walking on, I came to the parade of shops. Abdul's Videos was on the corner. I wanted to rent some videos, but suddenly I didn't know if I should go in, or even if I could. I doubted my dad had remembered to cancel his membership before leaving—but I wasn't sure what reception I'd get if I went in without him. It could be like the scene in *Mary Poppins* where the children found places weren't so welcoming when they went there alone. I couldn't resist the chance to inhale that video smell again. I pushed open the door and breathed deeply. It reminded me so much of happier times that tears started. I was about to back out when Abdul emerged from behind the counter. "Can I help you?" he asked. He gave me a curious look. He was used to seeing me as part of a double act and was having trouble placing me on my own. "You come in here with someone. Your father?"

"That's right. He's moved to America."

He shook his head sadly at the loss of a good customer. He paused for a moment, debating whether he could trust me. "Can you stick around for a while?"

There was nowhere else I wanted to be. "Sure."

"I need to go out for a moment. Do you think you could watch the shop? If anyone comes in, just tell them I'll be back soon." He pointed to the fridge full of Coke cans and the rack on the counter stacked with popcorn and chocolate bars. "Have a snack if you want." Also on the counter was a twelve-inch television with built-in video player. "I have one or two videos if you'd like to watch something." He went out. There was no doubt what I was going to pick first. A copy of *A Hard Day's Night* was on the shelf. Although the TV speaker was small and crackly, the opening clang of the title song took me back into the music I missed so much. As I heard the harmonies, twanging guitar, and frenzied bongo playing, it was too much for my famished soul. There were no customers around, so I didn't try to stop myself from breaking down in tears. I watched the film to the end and, still hungry for rock and roll, looked around for something else. I was disappointed to find the shop light on music films. The only other one Abdul had was *Tommy*. Although The Who might make the bottom part of my top ten groups list, I've never been a fan of this film. It takes surrealism too far. I'd like to have been at the meeting where Ken Russell asked his technical crew about the logistics of making half a ton of baked beans flood out of a television screen. Not all the music is the best either. Obviously, 'Pinball Wizard' and 'See Me, Feel Me' are great songs, but a rock opera has the same issue as any other opera. Even Mozart wrote pedestrian music while he concentrated on telling the story. *Tommy* is no exception. There are parts where the characters speak-sing dialogue to each other without much of a tune. I used the fast forward button to take me to the best bits.

As the end credits of *Tommy* rolled, there was still no sign of Abdul coming back. He had a flexible idea of how long a moment was. I had to consider what to watch next. Despite what the boys at school thought, I did have an interest in seeing what a woman looked like with no clothes on, so I chose a video from the top shelf. My heart was beating fast as I took the tape out of its box and pushed it into the slot on the front of the machine. Although video nasties were the main target for moral crusaders, some of them were keen to remind us porn could also deprave and corrupt. What hideous perversions was I about to see? The screen buzzed and popped for a few seconds. After some electronic music playing at the wrong speed, the film opened on a scene of a giant black plastic telephone, about six feet tall and eight wide. A young woman came on, grinning broadly. She was wearing a red one-piece swimsuit and had the look fashionable in the 1980s—a mane of bleach blonde hair, wide shoulders, large breasts, and a body which looked toned instead of starved. She strutted towards the telephone and climbed onto it. After crawling to the top, she moved her hips up and down a few times in a vaguely masturbatory way. She climbed down, flashed her perfect teeth at the camera again, and went off. The lights faded on the giant phone and came back up on a giant plastic guitar. The same woman came on, climbed up the guitar and gyrated a little before climbing down. I pressed the fast forward to see if anything more interesting happened later in the film. The only thing that changed was the plastic object. After she'd climbed down from the final piece of apparatus, the film stopped. No credits. No closing address from the woman giving any context for what we'd seen. Just a blank screen. I felt righteous indignation. How dare anyone charge people to watch stuff like this? I'd put on the video in good faith, expecting to be depraved and corrupted, not bored and irritated.

When the watered-down beer fails to make you drunk, you move on to something stronger. It was time to have my mind raped by a genuine video nasty, but which one to choose? Unlike the adult films, which were all on the top shelf, the nasties were scattered throughout the shop. I asked Abdul later why he didn't put films of the same genre together. He said, if he did that, the comedy fans would go straight to that section, the science fiction buffs would only look in one place. As it was, everyone browsed the whole shop and often saw something interesting, even if it wasn't the sort of movie they normally watched. It was good for business and for the customers' well-being. Abdul believed people got jaded if they only watched one type of film. I walked around the shop, looking at the box covers which were familiar from spreads in the *Daily*

*Mail.* A lot of the titles sounded like they'd been written by exasperated parents: *Don't Answer the Phone; Don't Go in the Woods; Don't Go Near the Park; Don't Look in the Basement;* just sit still and don't do anything. Other titles stressed the word 'house': *House on Straw Hill; The House by the Cemetery; The House on the Edge of the Park; The Last House on the Left.* This was to shake you out of the comforting belief that you had to visit Castle Dracula or the mad scientist's lab for bad things to happen. The evil could come for you right there in your own home. The titles I found most disturbing were: *SS Hell Camp; Gestapo's Last Orgy; SS Experiment Camp.* The covers showed Teutonic women with their breasts straining against black leather SS uniforms. My dad had told me enough about the Third Reich for me to know there was nothing sexy about Nazis. Later on, I kind of understood, even if I didn't approve. There's a fascination in a lawless world. Imagine knowing you could commit any act of sex or violence with no consequences. The Third Reich was one of the worst examples of humanity with all constraints removed. Another favourite word in titles was 'cannibal': *Cannibal Apocalypse; Cannibal Ferox; Cannibal Holocaust; Cannibal Man; Cannibal Terror.* I never knew there was such widespread interest in people eating each other. I decided if I ever made a video nasty, I'd call it *Don't Go Into The House of the Nazi Cannibal.* With a name like that, it couldn't fail.

The titles were one way of drawing in the punters. There were also the box covers. Vivid red letters standing out against black backgrounds. Blood dripping off knives and scantily clad women tied up. Two covers were featured most often in the press. The first was *Cannibal Holocaust,* which featured a painting of a dark-skinned man with straggly black hair chowing down on a loop of intestine, presumably human. His face was such a mask of wide-eyed delight at how delicious it was I couldn't help but laugh. Characters in comics had the same expression on being confronted with a plate of sausage and mash. I never laughed at the cover of *The Driller Killer,* which showed a man screaming in agony as an electric drill entered his temple. Blood flowed down his forehead, pooled in his right eye socket, and ran in two streams down his cheek. I always felt a bit sick when I saw it so, obviously, I was keen to watch the film. One campaigner had described it as having scenes so violent they could change someone's entire life. Given how unhappy I was at school, I liked the idea of having my entire life changed. This was the film I chose to take my video nasty virginity.

My heart was thumping again as I put the cassette into the machine. I was exposing myself to the scourge of my generation. It was like deliberately catching the plague. I didn't know how these films were structured. Would there be a plot of any kind or just wall-to-wall gore? Given the cover art, I expected the drill to get to work on people immediately. The first scene, however, showed the protagonist going into a church, possibly looking for redemption, but running away after being spooked by an old man. No drills were involved. The main character turned out to be a struggling artist trying to finish his latest painting, arguing with his girlfriend, and being driven crazy by the punk band in his building playing at all hours. Haunted by visions of his absent father, he suspected his dad might have become a vagrant and worked out his feelings of abandonment by killing tramps and winos—Oedipus by proxy. If ever a movie was going to turn me into a killer, it was this one. I could sympathise with his feelings. My dad hadn't become a tramp or a wino, but I could have roamed the university campus, killing visiting professors to take revenge on him for leaving me. As a depiction of descent into madness, the film worked well, but it was like seeing interpretive dance during a football match. No matter how good it is, it's not what we came for. I'd been promised life-changing violence and didn't get any.

After Abdul returned, I walked back to school, killing no one on the way.

# CHAPTER THIRTEEN

T HAT'S HOW IT STARTED. ABDUL LEFT me alone in his shop. When he came back, he found everything in order—all the videos still on the shelves, all the money still in the till. Although I was hungry, only one small chocolate bar and one can of Coke had gone. I'd proved myself trustworthy so he asked if I would like to come back the next day and become a part-time employee. He agreed to pay me two pounds for every hour I spent in the shop. Even in those days, it sounded like slave labour, but I'd have done it for free. It wasn't about the money. It was about having a new bolt hole. The time I'd spent at home would now be spent at Abdul's Videos. On my first official day of work, he showed me how to log each rental in the leather-bound ledger, take the money, and hand over the video in a pink library case. It wasn't a highly skilled job, and I was fully trained in ten minutes. He went out again, confident I could run the business in his absence. As he left, he said the most important thing for me to do was familiarise myself with the stock. As that meant watching a lot of videos, I wasn't complaining. Abdul wasn't merely a guy who ran a video shop: he was a video librarian. He prided himself on having seen every film on his shelves. If I was going to be his number two, I'd have to do the same. He got to know his regulars. If he saw someone looking unsure what to choose, he'd go over to them with a selection of videos fanned out on his forearm. "I remember you enjoyed *Local Hero* a few weeks ago. You might like *Educating Rita*—it has a similar sense of humour. Have you seen *The King of Comedy*? It's not a comedy, despite the title, but I think you'll appreciate the cleverness of the script." Faced with this level of personal service, few people walked out of the shop empty handed. Abdul's Videos did well, to begin with.

Given how haphazard I was at school about showing up and doing any work, it was surprising I became a model employee of Abdul's Videos. I needed this place, so I arrived on time. I did everything Abdul said. I always had *some* Coke and chocolate from behind the counter but didn't go overboard.

When I was there, Abdul often took the opportunity to go out and . . . well, I'm not sure what he was doing. Maybe he was meeting with video distributers. Perhaps he was spending time with his family. If the two of us were there at the same time, we talked a bit. We didn't have much in common except movies, so we talked about those. There was a certain amount of trying to catch each other out. "The other day, I was watching the final film to feature Paul Henreid . . ."

"Oh, you mean *Exorcist II: The Heretic*. I was watching Charlie Chaplin's last film . . ."

"*A Countess From New York.*"

"No, *The Gentleman Tramp.*"

"Would you call it a real movie?"

Other times, we were two fan boys, debating which was the best Bond film or the best adaptation of a Raymond Chandler book. Occasionally, we talked about other things. He was born in India, but as Muslims in a largely Hindu part of the country, his family had faced discrimination. Coming over to the UK, they'd also encountered hostility, but his father had established himself in the local community by being so useful. He opened a shop selling everything. In those days, shops run by native Britons often opened at nine in the morning and closed at five in the evening. Some of them even had the nerve to shut for an hour at lunchtime. Abdul's dad opened at seven in the morning so folks could buy a newspaper and cigarettes on their way to work. He also stayed open until eleven at night to cater for people who'd underestimated how many bottles they'd need for a quiet evening in. He never touched alcohol himself but had no religious or moral qualms about making large sums of money from it. If a customer asked for something he didn't have, he always said, "I can order it for you and make sure it's here for you next time." This put the customer under a certain obligation to come back. After a while, it didn't occur to the customer to go anywhere else. When videos started becoming popular in the early 1980s, Abdul's dad put a small rack of films at the back of his shop. Even though he rented them out for only 50p a night, videos soon joined cigarettes and alcohol as the most lucrative part of his business. Abdul saw videos as the future. On leaving school, he borrowed money from his dad to open a shop of his own. He stocked it with videos and waited for the people to come. He used his dad's trick for fostering loyalty. If a customer asked for a film not on the shelves, the answer was never, "I don't have it," but, "I can order it for you," or, if that wasn't possible, "I have a couple I think you'll enjoy just as much." Abdul's dream was to go back to his hometown in India and show everyone how well he'd done in England. There was a girl there he'd always fancied. If she was still single, he hoped she'd be impressed by the rich businessman and agree to marry him. We also talked a bit about politics. Mrs Thatcher once warned the Australian foreign minister against letting as many Asians into Australia as had been allowed into the UK. Nevertheless, she loved people like Abdul: those who started their own businesses and became successful through hard work rather than asking the state for money. He loved her right back for cutting taxes and reducing bureaucracy. From what he was saying, it sounded like Mrs Thatcher was doing some things that were . . . good. It went against everything I'd grown up believing.

Although Abdul was undoubtedly the boss, he picked up immediately that barking orders would not get the best out of me. Instead, he asked me questions with only one possible answer. "What do you think about putting the new tapes on the shelf?"

He got mad at me only once. It was one afternoon after he'd gone out, leaving me in charge. A kid with curly blond hair and a silver front tooth came in. He looked about sixteen. "Where's the Paki?" he asked.

I hated him immediately for talking about Abdul like this and feigned ignorance. "The who?" I asked.

"Fat Paki with the tache. He's normally here."

"I think you're talking about the owner and manager," I said, coldly. "He has stepped out, but I can help you with anything you need." He spent a few minutes looking around. From the way his eyes kept darting up to the top shelf, I knew what sort of video he wanted. He picked up *The Devil in Miss Jones II* and brought it to the counter. "Are you eighteen?" I asked him.

"Yes, are you?"

I wasn't so didn't answer. "I'm going to have to see some ID."

He made a show of patting his pockets. "The one day I don't bring it. Tell you what, let me have the movie now and I'll show you my ID when I bring it back."

"Sorry."

"Oh, go on, mate."

"It's nothing to do with me. It's the law."

"The Paki lets me have what I want."

"So maybe you should treat him with more respect."

"He's still a—"

I didn't let him finish. There was a red button under the counter. I pressed it and an alarm sounded. "It's also ringing at the police station," I lied loudly over the noise. "When they find out you've been trying to rent porn without ID, you'll be appearing in your own prison drama. You'll have the starring role as some serial killer's little puppy."

I don't know how much of this he heard, but he ran for the door and crashed into Abdul, who was coming in. "Sorry," said the kid. I had at least taught him some manners. He scampered off down the street.

Abdul readied himself for a hundred-yard sprint. "Did he nick anything?" he yelled at me. The videos were his babies and he'd fight to the death anyone who tried to steal them.

I switched off the alarm. "No."

He looked relieved he didn't have to give chase. "Why the alarm?"

"He's not the type we want in here."

"Anyone who rents videos is the type we want in here," he said. I told him the full story, including the word the kid had used. I expected Abdul to praise me for defending him. His eyes darkened and I was scared of him for the first time since I was a boy. He kept his voice steady as he asked, "Do you think Harry Carpenter is a racist?"

Harry Carpenter was a BBC sports presenter, but I'd never met the man and didn't know his views on anything. "Not that I'm aware," I replied.

"I was watching Wimbledon last night, and I heard Harry Carpenter say, 'Let's see how the Brits got on today.' Was he being racist?"

I tried to think instead of simply saying what Abdul wanted to hear. "I don't think so."

"So, it's okay to call a British person a Brit, but it's wrong to call someone from Pakistan a Paki. What's the difference? They're both abbreviations. I'm not from Pakistan, so the worst you can say is the kid's geography is a bit off."

I couldn't let this go. "The difference is Harry Carpenter didn't *mean* it to be offensive. The kid was deliberately using a racist slur to put you down."

Abdul saw my heart was in the right place and calmed down. "I could say no one's allowed in my shop unless they're the same religion as me, vote the same as me, support the same football team as me. Or I could say, come in, everyone's welcome. Racists' money is as good as anyone else's. Someday, I'm going to have Abdul's Videos in every town in the world. When that kid sees me driving around in a Rolls Royce with my beautiful wife beside me, it'll be a bigger slap in the face than kicking him out of my shop." He picked up the video the kid had dropped on the counter. "Have you seen this?" I shook my head. "It has some attempt at a story as Miss Jones bargains with the Devil to be allowed out of hell. It tries to be a comedy, but the jokes are no good, so it uses breasts to keep the audience's attention. The kid would not have been scarred for life by seeing a few boobies. I know you were trying to do the right thing, but don't do it again. It's our job to bring customers in and keep them coming, not chase them away."

"Sorry."

He handed me the video. "Your punishment is to watch this."

I sat behind the counter and put on the film. The jokes were terrible, but the breasts were nice, so it wasn't much of a punishment.

# CHAPTER FOURTEEN

Abdul's shop was on the corner. Halfway down the street, an old electrical goods store had been sitting empty for months. The place was open again. A large orange banner spanned the whole frontage. In red letters, it announced RITZ VIDEO. I stopped to peer in through the window and was immediately concerned. The shop was three times the size of Abdul's. They had a life-sized cardboard cut-out of Arnold Schwarzenegger as Conan. Bins full of popcorn and water bottles were dotted around the floor. Every video I could think of, plus many I'd never heard of, were on the shelves. There were multiple copies of *Return of the Jedi*, *Octopussy*, and *Superman III*. If Abdul's was a video library, this was a video supermarket.

Abdul was straightening up the last remaining shelf of Betamax videos as I came in. "Have you seen it?" I asked. He knew what I meant and nodded. "Aren't you worried?"

He smiled. "Why don't you go in there and ask whoever's behind the counter when the next zombie film is coming in?"

I was worried someone might have seen me in Abdul's and I'd be arrested for spying, but I went into Ritz. A pretty girl in a yellow t-shirt behind the counter gave me a look that said, "I'm out of your league—don't take up more of my time than absolutely necessary."

I asked her Abdul's question. She gave me another look. This one said, "You are such a geek." She called across the shop floor. "Tim, this . . . gentleman," the word clearly left a bad taste in her mouth, "wants to know about zombie films or something."

A lad not much older came over. He had a light brown mullet and a face lumpy with acne. He was proudly wearing a badge saying MANAGER on the front of his yellow t-shirt. I was about to start quizzing him when Abdul stepped up. I hadn't realised he'd followed me in. Who was minding his shop? Dispensing with small talk, Abdul asked Tim, "Which do you think is better, *Zombi 2* or *Zombie Flesh Eaters*?"

I must say, the lad did a good job of pretending to consider the matter. "Personally, I prefer *Zombi 2*."

"Interesting," said Abdul, "because they're alternative titles for the same film. Which do you think is the best one of *The Gates of Hell* trilogy?"

"They all have their good points," stammered Tim. The people who worked for him were watching and smirking at the boss's embarrassment.

"They should never have tried to make one without Lucio Fulci directing."

"No, definitely not," agreed Tim.

"It's a good thing they didn't, then. The third film in the trilogy is his best work since *The House by the Cemetery*."

"Absolutely."

"Or, to put it another way, it is *The House by the Cemetery*."

Tim was blushing scarlet. Abdul decided Tim had suffered enough and we left. "That's why people will always come to my place," he told me, as he unlocked his door, and we went back in.

He left me alone for the rest of the afternoon. When he came back at five in the evening, I had just enough time to walk back to school in time for tea. Mr Hamilton did sometimes wander around the dining room, checking who was there, so I normally showed up for meals even if I didn't eat anything. On my way out of the video shop, I ran into Jason. His hostility to me as a gay predator biding my time before sexually assaulting him was replaced by curiosity. "What are you doing in there?" he asked.

"I work there."

For the first time, I'd said something that interested him. "Could you get me some videos?" he asked.

"Maybe."

"*The Evil Dead*, stuff like that?"

"We've got all the video nasties."

His interest wasn't too surprising. The three tests of manliness at our school were: how much alcohol you'd drunk; how far you'd gone with a girl; and which video nasties you'd seen. From the back row of the classroom, I heard things like, "I've seen *Night of the Demon*."

"That's nothing. I've seen *Night of the Bloody Apes*. Believe me, that was a much worse night."

Jason and I fell into uneasy step together as we walked back to school. As soon as we were inside the gates, he ran off before anyone saw us together. For once, I was glad I'd seen him, as he'd given me an idea.

Abdul's shop was one bolt hole. I had almost given up on finding one at school. Our house was a rambling old building but, wherever I went, there were people. Finally, I found a room on the top floor that was used by the cleaners. The bottles of the chlorine-based disinfectant which gave the house its distinctive smell were stacked up against one wall. There was a big sink for emptying out buckets of dirty water. I finally had a place where I could wash in private. It wasn't big enough for me to have a bath in, but I could stand naked in front of it and wash myself down. The buckets and mops were stored against the opposite wall. Next to the room was a small cubicle with a toilet in it. Just a toilet, a basin, and a stack of toilet roll packets. It wasn't the most salubrious place I'd ever seen, but I knew I'd found my school bolt hole. No one used this place after the cleaners went home at midday. Crucially, it locked from the inside. I had my private space where I did the things no one else could ever see. I hid some of my old music magazines behind the toilet rolls and started spending every spare moment there.

Try as I might, I couldn't find any way of sleeping there. I spread toilet roll packs over the floor. They were soft enough but, even if I lay diagonally, there wasn't enough room for me to stretch out. I'd have been curled into a tighter ball than I was in my bed.

If I stayed in my bolt hole until thirteen minutes past ten, I could run to the dormitory, change into my pyjamas, and try to be in bed before anyone noticed me.

# CHAPTER FIFTEEN

A FTER TEA ON SATURDAY, THOSE OF US WHO hadn't gone home for the weekend were left to our own devices. The more dedicated pupils used this time to do extra work. Others set up games of chess or cards. Mr Hamilton often put a couple of video cassettes by the player in the TV room. My dad would have approved of his choices. They tended to be classics or worthy foreign films.

The next Saturday, the boys were fighting over whether to watch *It Happened One Night* or *La Grande Illusion* without showing much enthusiasm for either. I stood up at the front of the room. "What are you doing, poof?" one of them wanted to know.

I ignored him and did my best impression of Neville Chamberlain. Holding aloft a copy of *The Last House on the Left*, I announced, "I have in my hand a video nasty which will restore peace." No one could object to watching a video nasty, as it would make them look squeamish, which was taken as another sign of being gay. I continued my introduction. "It features David Hess, who is also a songwriter and co-wrote 'Speedy Gonzales,' a big hit for Pat Boone." I saw a room full of blank faces. None of them knew who Pat Boone was. "He also co-wrote 'I Got Stung' for Elvis Presley." This earned a flicker of recognition. They had at least heard of Elvis. "He did the music for this film, as well. As you listen to the plaintive folk singing on the soundtrack, remember it's the same guy who's wreaking murderous havoc on screen."

I pushed the cassette into the player, and we watched the film. Some people left as soon as it was over, but I wanted to recreate the experience of Mr Brownlow's evenings at the Forum, as far as I could with a bunch of schoolkids. I asked if anyone had any comments. Some of the guys just enjoyed the violence and breasts on display. Others were surprisingly thoughtful. A lad called Paul said he found the film moral in its own way. The rape scene was carefully shot so it wasn't a turn-on but sad and depressing. A sixth-form girl called Jackie, who was sitting at the back, remarked that, even at her lowest point, the woman being raped had more dignity than the dumb thug who was committing the act. I agreed and said, "It's a much more moral film than *Straw Dogs*, for example, where the woman seems unsure during the rape if she wants to go along with it or not. Here, there's never any doubt Mari hates every second of it. The ending is also more plausible. At the end of *Straw Dogs*, Dustin Hoffman's character takes out all the bad guys and proclaims triumphantly, 'I got 'em all!' When Mari's parents take their revenge on the rapist and his gang, there's no celebration, only despair that they've been forced down to the criminals' level."

The talk went on for over an hour and was the best part of the night. It highlighted something I've noticed about video nasties: discussing them is often more interesting than watching them.

After the success of the first one, we had a video nasty evening every Saturday. It made my life more bearable. It didn't make me the most popular boy in the school overnight, but it changed the narrative. People came to me with suggestions for films I could show rather than comments about my sexuality.

The best talk we had was after a viewing of *Cannibal Holocaust*. I'm generally opposed to censorship, but I do have sympathy with those who'd like to ban Italian cannibal films because of their tendency to include real animal deaths. To me, it's obscene for an animal's experience of life to be over for the sake of a mere film. I was interested to hear the other boys' views. Fortunately, the guys who saw compassion for animals as yet another sign of being gay left the room quickly. Some of those who remained tried to defend the indefensible. One boy said we were being hypocritical. We all ate meat but preferred the unpleasant realities of its production to stay hidden behind the abattoir walls. He had a point. My dad had never expressed any opinions on the ethics of meat. He rarely ate it but that was because he couldn't be bothered to prepare it. Consequently, there had never been much meat in my diet. I stopped eating it altogether soon afterwards and didn't miss it at all. I came back with the argument that, even if it's part of real life, why was it included in a movie? It was pushing animal slaughter into the realm of entertainment, where it didn't belong. Another lad made the point that the easiest way to present something on film is to do it. If you want to show a man walking through Hyde Park, you can build an elaborate set in the studio, but it's easier and cheaper to put the actor in the real Hyde Park and let him walk. By the same token, if you want to show a turtle being killed, the easiest and cheapest way of doing it is to kill a turtle. I shared with them what Abdul had told me about this film. Director Ruggero Deodato had been keen to push the idea of *cinéma-vérité* to the limit. He wanted the audience to believe the people killed by the cannibal tribe really died. He even made the actors sign an agreement to disappear and not be seen in the media for a year after the film's release. The animal deaths helped put doubts into people's minds. If Deodato was sufficiently crazy to kill animals for real, maybe he was insane enough to do the same to people.

The UK's Director of Public Prosecutions put together a list of official video nasties, thus creating a convenient must-see list for horror fans. From my bolt hole behind the counter in Abdul's shop, I worked my way through the list, picking the ones which would spark most debate to take into school. Abdul also subscribed to *Video World* and *Video—the magazine*. When I wasn't watching videos, I was reading about them. I came close to Abdul's level of knowledge, at least as far as the nasties were concerned. These were the films that most people wanted to know about. The tabloid outrage was generating lots of free publicity. One man came up to the counter with the boxes for *Cannibal Holocaust* and *Cannibal Ferox*. "Which one of these is better?" he asked.

I knew this would require a lengthy answer. I wished I'd taken up smoking so I could roll a cigarette like my dad would have done. As it was, I stepped from behind the counter so the man could appreciate my illustrative hand gestures. "The cinematography in *Holocaust* is more interesting. There's an effective contrast between the multiple camera set-ups of the main film and the handheld material of the film within a film." It was a clumsy way of describing it, but I didn't know the term 'found footage' in those days. "The best you can say about the cinematography in *Ferox* is that it's workmanlike. The music in *Holocaust* is excellent. The main theme is a gorgeous concerto for guitar and orchestra in G major. To be honest, it's far too good for a film like this. It was written by Riz Ortolani, who had a habit of casting his pearls before swine. His song 'More' featured in *Mondo Cane*, thus allowing that grubby little film to call itself Oscar-nominated. As for *Ferox*, there's a doom-laden musical motif running through it, which has more than a hint of Cream's 'White Room' about it. The main theme sounds like it belongs in some show from the seventies, probably one where a cop discovers his ex-wife is the new precinct chief with hilarious consequences. My main issue with *Ferox*, however, is it's based on a flawed premise. It's the story of an academic who goes into the Amazon jungle to prove cannibalism no longer exists. How's she going to do that unless she visits every last inch of the place? I went for a walk in the woods the other day and I didn't see a badger. Can I therefore conclude badgers do not exist?"

I must have inherited some of my dad's talent as a compelling speaker, because the man let me get through all this. Only when I paused for breath did he ask, "What are you going on about, mate?

Which one of these films is better?"

"You should ask which of these films is worse. *Holocaust* shows a woman impaled on a spike. *Ferox* shows a woman hung up by her breasts."

"All the violence is against women?"

I didn't like the way he asked this, but if Abdul insisted on serving racists, I guessed he felt the same about misogynists. I put him straight. "Not all. It also doesn't go well for you if you're a turtle or a penis. The cannibals' machete makes short work of them too."

"I'll take both," he said.

# CHAPTER SIXTEEN

M R HAMILTON'S VOICE CALLED MY NAME from the door to the cube room. "Phone," he said, before adding, "but you shouldn't be taking calls during prep."

I went along the corridor to the phone. I almost didn't recognise the voice asking, "Are you free on Saturday afternoon?"

"Abdul?"

"Of course. Well, are you?"

"Sure. What time?"

"Two o'clock."

"I'll be there."

It was only when I was in school assembly on Saturday morning and heard Mr Wilson asking to see everyone in the cricket teams that I realised I was double-booked. Something strange happened during the summer term. I calculated I'd pushed my luck far enough and I did need to go to a cricket practice. With no possibility of doing anything else, I tried playing the game. It turned out I was quite good. My dad never played sport and I don't know what my mother did in her younger days, but I had inherited hand eye coordination from somewhere. When I swung a bat at a ball, it often connected. When I threw a ball, it went in roughly the right direction. At the same time, several members of the cricket team went down with mumps. I didn't have much of an immune system but my policy of avoiding my fellows whenever possible meant I escaped a lot of the illnesses that went around. Mr Wilson was faced with a dilemma. He couldn't stand me and would have preferred to put the headmaster's cat in the team, but both the first and second elevens had matches that Saturday. He was in danger of not having twenty-two people who could stand up. It went against his most deeply held principles, but he picked me for the second eleven. It says something about the standard of play in the school that a pale, skinny kid who did everything possible to avoid sports made the team. The novelty of it should have made me remember it, but I'd agreed to Abdul's request without thinking.

"I can't play," I remarked casually to the captain, as he gathered with the rest of the team after assembly.

"What do you mean, you can't play?" he demanded.

"Which word did you not understand?" I asked.

"Come and tell that to Mr Wilson."

We went to where Mr Wilson was standing. I told him, "My boss called me last night and said I had to work this afternoon."

"You have a school commitment this afternoon."

"I'd rather be expelled from the school than fired from my job."

There was a delicious moment as I saw genuine bafflement in his eyes. If I didn't care about the school's ultimate punishment, there wasn't much he could do to me. "What's your work?" he asked.

I didn't want to tell him in case he had some notion of phoning Abdul and persuading him to release me for the afternoon. "I'm head of you don't need to know that at the none of your business corporation," I said in a faultlessly polite voice.

The captain was still annoyed with me, but the rest of the team laughed. Mr Wilson looked at them nervously. The guys who were good at sports gravitated to the PE teacher. He didn't want to look like he couldn't take a joke in front of his people. He smiled briefly before falling back on one of the clichés teachers learn at training college. "I . . . expect you to be there."

I loved the uncertainty in his voice and took full advantage. "Well, stop expecting me to be there," I said, without a trace of deference, "because there's not the faintest chance." I turned to the rest of the team. "Hope the game goes well, guys." I walked out of the hall and went to my first lesson.

# CHAPTER SEVENTEEN

THE VIDEO RECORDINGS ACT WAS PASSED IN 1984. It was rare for a Private Member's Bill to jump through all the hoops needed for it to become law, but Mrs Thatcher pulled some strings to ease the bill's passage. The act stated any video offered for sale or hire had to be submitted to the British Board of Film Classification and given a certificate. Anything too graphic in terms of sex or violence would be refused a certificate and no longer legally available. The act achieved its aim of taking video nasties off the shelves.

Abdul felt personally betrayed by Mrs Thatcher. She'd encouraged him to go into business, before taking away a significant part of his livelihood. He was like a pub landlord hearing Thatcher had outlawed beer. He removed the nasties from display but didn't throw them out. Maybe he couldn't bear to let them go completely. They stayed in a plastic box behind the counter.

By the time I was in the sixth form, morning lessons were interspersed with study periods. The headmaster made it clear this was not free time and talked darkly about what would happen to anyone who left the school grounds during these periods. I knew all the side entrances and was confident in my ability to sneak out without anyone seeing. If Abdul wanted me in the morning, I wasn't going to disappoint him.

On one such morning, a man came in. He briefly looked over the titles on the shelves and walked up to the counter. "You've had your balls cut off," he remarked.

I knew exactly what he meant. "Under the guise of protecting children, the government has dictated what can and cannot be enjoyed by adults in the privacy of their own homes."

"You don't approve?" he asked.

"I've a certain fondness for them. They've made my life at school more bearable."

"He rents these films out to school children?"

"No, I take them into school and . . ." Something told me to stop talking about that. I asked myself what Abdul would do at this point. "We still have some great horror films. *Friday the 13th* hasn't been banned. It surprised some it didn't make the official list of nasties, but here it is. One or two trims might have been made, but there's still enough to satisfy most gore fans. You could always try something a bit more classical like *The Exorcist* or *Rosemary's Baby.*"

He shook his head. "It's not the same, is it? Listen, I've been coming in here for a long time." I hadn't seen him before, but that didn't prove anything. Abdul stayed open until half past eleven every evening to catch the people who wanted to rent a video on their way home from the pub. Even I couldn't be out of school then so there were a lot of regulars I'd never met. "I'm good friends with Abdul." I had no way of knowing if this was true. "He sometimes shows me the private stuff he keeps behind the counter." I was interested to hear this. Did Abdul have a secret stash of porn more interesting than the stuff I'd seen so far? "Let's see what you've got back there. I'll pay double."

I put the plastic box on the counter. "Nice one!" he said, looking through the forbidden titles. He picked out *Anthropophagus—The Beast*, a clunkily acted film, in which the special effects ranged from horrific to laughable. I processed the rental in the normal way. The man went out, looking happy.

As I was walking back to school, I saw Mr Wilson driving past. He'd done whatever was necessary to stop his car being a death trap and it was now back on the road. I ducked behind a tree and wasn't sure if he'd seen me. Sneaking back into school through the service truck entrance, I went to my next lesson and didn't think any more about it until lunch time. Everyone in the house was milling about outside the dining hall when I felt a tap on my shoulder. I turned to find myself face to stomach with Mr Wilson. He was trying the trick some teachers had learned of standing too close. It was supposed to be intimidating but made me think he had a substantial belly for someone who taught sports. "What were you doing outside?" he asked, without any civilities.

"Taking a little air," I replied. "Clearing my head from all the studying I do all the time."

My housemates sensed something was happening and gathered round a bit more closely. "I saw you," said Mr. Wilson.

"And I saw you." Playing to the crowd, I added, "It was the highlight of my day." This got a chuckle, which irritated Mr Wilson.

"What if you'd been run over?" he asked.

I couldn't believe he was asking such a stupid question. I was seventeen. I no longer needed a responsible adult's help crossing the road. "What if the Martians had landed?" I responded, thinking that equally probable.

"Your parents are paying us to look after you. If I see you outside again, don't be surprised if something happens to you."

He expected me to be cowed by this threat and he started to walk away. "What do you think could happen to me?" I demanded, loudly enough to make him stop and turn. "Put me on detention, I won't go. Have me suspended, I'll be glad of the holiday. If you get me expelled, I'll be so grateful, I'll marry you."

This earned me a gasp from the other boys followed by a big laugh. Mr Wilson stood there, looking gratifyingly baffled. The bell rang and we all filed into lunch, leaving him alone. I assumed the matter was closed but that's what got me expelled. After everything else I'd done, I was surprised this particular straw broke the camel's back. A public declaration that the school rules did not apply to me was a step too far. As I entered the language lab for the first lesson of the afternoon, the Mr Beaumont waved at me. "The headmaster wants to see you."

I went to the headmaster's study without any sense of doom. After I'd sat down in front of his desk, he said, "You seem to spend more time out of school than in it. Mr Wilson tells me you said something about having a job."

I didn't see much point in denying it. "That's right."

"Why do you want a job? Don't we fill your time enough?"

"More than enough," I responded but didn't want to explain to him the concept of the bolt hole. I fell back on the most plausible explanation. "It's not about time: it's about money."

"If you'd rather work than go to school, that's your choice, but we don't take anyone on a part-time basis. You'll leave the school at the end of this term." Standing up, he offered me his hand. Although he was ultimately responsible for the school being the way it was, I had no particular quarrel with him, so I shook his hand and left the room. In a way, I would have preferred to leave immediately, vanish, and leave people wondering where I'd gone. Instead, I became the school's dead man walking. People were talking about a next term I'd never see. The good thing was it gave me time to prepare. The school would contact my dad to tell him what had happened. He wouldn't acknowledge them in any way. Even though I was at least partially an adult, the school might be reluctant to push me out of the gate with no visible means of support. There could be some nonsense about giving me over to the care of a responsible relative. While I was grateful to my Aunty Joy for the postal orders on my birthday, I hadn't seen her in more than ten years. She was a middle-aged spinster. I was a young man with no great love of tea and scones. She liked classical music, occasionally listening to The Seekers when she was feeling wild. I couldn't see myself fitting into her life.

The obvious place for me to go was Abdul's Videos. What was to stop me putting a mattress behind the counter? I could live happily on popcorn, chocolate, and Coke. I'd have no shortage of entertainment. Soon, my knowledge of the stock would equal Abdul's across all genres of videos. I could sell the idea to Abdul as his opportunity to stay open twenty-four hours a day. How many times have you lain in bed at two in the morning, wide awake, wishing you could rent a video to while away the restless hours? If I slept behind the counter, the bell above the door would wake me up. I could serve the customer and go back to sleep. I'd never have to leave the shop. It would be the ultimate bolt hole.

The next day, I left the school grounds through the main gate in the middle of morning lessons. There was no longer a reason to pretend I had any interest in the school routine. I walked towards the parade of shops. While I was still two hundred yards away, I saw something was wrong. The front of Abdul's Videos was normally covered with posters for the latest films. All of them had been taken down and swirls of whitewash had been roughly painted on the insides of the windows. A block of timber was nailed over the front door. There wasn't a notice anywhere to explain why the shop had closed.

I wanted to stand in the street and scream Abdul's name, hoping he'd come and rescue me. I had an idea. Maybe his shop had been absorbed into Ritz Video down the road. He'd sat down with Tim and they'd decided there was no point being in competition when they could work together. Abdul would be standing behind the counter in his new role as joint manager and would be delighted to welcome me onto the team.

I went down the road. Even on a weekday morning, the Ritz was thriving—posters in the windows, customers browsing the shelves. The young people who worked there were laughing over some shared joke as they put video boxes on the shelves and filled the bins with packs of popcorn and M&Ms. Everything looked wrong. I couldn't imagine myself in one of those yellow t-shirts with the company logo over my left nipple. The popcorn and chocolate belonged behind the counter within easy reach of the bolt hole. Nevertheless, I went up to the counter. There was barely enough room to stand behind it. I couldn't see anywhere I might lay my bed. A lad I'd never seen before asked, "Yes, pal?" I winced. Abdul would never have spoken to a customer like this.

"Is Abdul around?" I asked. It suddenly sounded like a bizarre question to ask out of the blue.

"Who?" asked the lad.

"He used to run the other video shop down the road."

"Oh, you mean the . . ." At the last moment, he changed what he was going to say to, ". . . the Asian guy. Why would he be here?"

"His shop's closed down. I thought maybe—"

He grinned. "Good, isn't it? It means all his old customers will come here."

"Do you know what happened?"

He shook his head. Tim the manager walked past and heard what we were saying. "He couldn't compete. I mean, look at this place. He was stuck in the past. His shop was a shit hole." He had mispronounced 'bolt,' but I let it go.

A third lad joined in. "I heard he was up to something illegal. The cops came and shut the place down."

"Illegal?" I queried.

"We burned all our video nasties here," said Tim. "I toasted a marshmallow over *The Evil Dead*."

I couldn't spend another second with people who had no respect for either Abdul or video nasties. I left the shop and looked up and down the street, willing Abdul to be there. I wanted him to appear and take me with him, wherever he was going. I'd happily have gone to India and persuaded his childhood sweetheart to marry him. Abdul was nowhere in sight, and I never saw him again.

It left me with the little problem of what to do with the rest of my life. I seriously considered walking into the Army recruitment office in town and presenting myself with just the clothes I stood up in. I have heard of other people who are natural rebels doing that. Kicking against authority becomes too exhausting, so they put themselves in a position where they can't do anything except say, "Yes, sir." I also liked the idea of marching into school for an old boys' reunion and showing Mr Wilson my sergeant's stripes. I was held back by the thought of how disappointed my dad would be if he found out. He'd scarcely have been more dismayed if I'd joined Thatcher's government.

I must admit this feeling of not belonging anywhere did make me ask if it was easier to end it all. It's a good thing I didn't have access to a gun. If I'd had a quick and painless way of going out, I might have taken that option. None of the other methods appealed. I could see myself leaping from a tall building and immediately regretting it, desperately trying to grab hold of something on the way down. I didn't want my last moments on earth to be ones of blind panic. Equally, I didn't like the idea of going to bed and swallowing all the pills I could find. Again, I could see myself having too much time for regrets as I lay there, hyper-alert to any changes in my body. Was the feeling in my stomach a touch of cramp or was it me starting to die? I entertained these thoughts for no more than a few minutes. I needed to escape, but not this way. With nowhere else to go, I went back to school.

I still went to the occasional class where I liked the teacher but spent most of my time in the house quiet room. As well as the national newspapers, there were a couple of local ones. I generally found these dull with their accounts of garden fetes and amateur theatre productions, but now I had a reason for reading them. I needed two things: a source of income and a place to stay. I often passed homeless people in town and usually gave them a few coins, trying to rack up karmic points so it wouldn't happen to me. I was sure I'd get no rest at all if I were on the streets—cold, uncomfortable, always afraid of being robbed or attacked. There was a real danger of this happening if I ran away from school without a plan. I didn't need anywhere fancy, just a bolt hole. I was happy to share a bathroom and kitchen. Six square feet of carpet where I could lie and listen to music was enough for me. I looked at the Accommodation for Rent and the Situations Vacant columns. The sums did not add up. I would have to work a hundred hours a week to afford a one room flat. How did anyone live in this town? I was becoming depressed about my prospects when I saw an advertisement for a job at a hotel in town. It wasn't my dream job: cleaning the rooms after the guests had checked out or left for the day. The role was that of a chambermaid but, in a spirit of equal opportunity drudgery, the ad made it clear both men and women could apply. The hours were eight to twelve in the morning. The pay wasn't great, but the words catching my attention were, 'Accommodation included.' I determined to become a chamberman or a chamberlad or whatever the male equivalent was. Once the decision had been made, the rest of my plan formed quickly.

I went into town, looking for a hairdresser's. I was sporting the flowing locks of Jim Morrison slash *Let It Be* era John Lennon— or as close as I could manage within the confines of a boarding school. It would have to change. I wanted to save as much money as possible, so I hoped the haircut I had in mind wouldn't cost too much. I sat down in a barber's chair and fifteen minutes later had a half-inch carpet of fuzz all over my head. My next trip was to the charity shop. I wanted a cheap suit that didn't fit too well.

The job advertisement had included a number to ring, but the first place I saw on emerging from the charity shop was the very hotel I planned to work at. I figured I'd save some time by going in. The front of the building tried to look like a Tudor coaching inn with its white panels and horizontal black beams. It was built around a courtyard which pretended to be where the horse was fed and watered while the rider enjoyed a slice of game pie and a tankard of ale. I'd seen the place being built from the ground up two years before, so I wasn't fooled. There were five doors leading from the courtyard. The one marked 'Reception' seemed the most promising. I walked up to the desk, where a middle-aged woman with her hair in a bun eyed me suspiciously. I looked too young to be checking into a hotel on my own, so was probably up to mischief. "Can I help you?" she asked, frostily.

"I was asked to come here about the job in the paper."

"Oh, yes?" she said, as if this might be plausible. "Who did you speak to?"

I frowned. "He did give me his name . . ."

"Mr Curry's in charge of that section."

"Yes, of course. Mr Curry. He's the person who asked me to come in. How could I forget that name? I fancied a curry after I spoke to him and went straight down my local Indian restaurant." I realised I was talking too much and shut up.

"He's doing interviews this afternoon. He asked you to come in this morning?"

"I might have misheard him. Some workmen were drilling in the road outside my window. I shouted at them to take five so I could talk to Mr Curry, but they were having none of it." I shut up again.

"I'll see if he's around. Take a seat." She pointed to a row of red padded chairs. I sat in the first one, keeping my back straight and with my hands at my sides.

Five minutes later, a harassed looking man with short grey hair and two days' growth of salt and pepper stubble hurried along the corridor. He was wearing a rumpled black suit, tie, and a white shirt with the top button undone. It was a look I came to associate with junior managers. "You wanted to see me?" he asked.

I stood to attention in front of him. I thought about saluting but decided that was going too far. Instead, I offered him my hand. "It's good to meet you, sir. We spoke about the job on the phone."

I knew I was taking a risk, but I'd seen enough of Abdul and my teachers to know a person at any level of responsibility has a thousand things to remember and always forgets some of them. He'd probably spoken to a hundred people on the phone, and I might have been one of them. It worked. "That's right," he said, nodding as he pretended to remember. He didn't have an office so led me into the hotel's restaurant where the smell was of mass-produced rather than good food. "Remind me which job you're interested in."

Given how much I was chancing my arm, I should have gone for broke and tried for a management position, but I told him it was the part-time housekeeper role.

"What experience do you have in this kind of work?"

The truth is, I had no experience of housework beyond running a cloth over video boxes. My dad never insisted I make my bed or tidy my room. As we never had visitors, there was no incentive to keep the house nice. He could work perfectly well with his feet on an unhoovered carpet. At school, the housework was done by the cleaners or not at all. "I've just come out of the Army," I said, running a hand across my boot scraper hair, "as you can see." I was hoping the cheap suit would make me look like I'd been demobbed in a hurry and put into whatever clothes were in the quartermaster's stores. "Unfortunately, my last blood pressure reading was a bit too high for the MO, and I was let go. For the last five years, I've been making my bed and cleaning the barracks to military standards. If it's good enough for Corporal Clark, I'm sure it's good enough for your guests."

He smiled. "I'm sure it is." He frowned, looking suspicious for the first time. "You've spent five years in the Army? You seem so young."

I should have thought of that. The Army doesn't normally take people on at the age of twelve. I could have tried fudging the issue by saying part of my military career was on a cadet scheme. I decided instead to show nothing but pleasure at the compliment. "Thank you, sir. Nice of you to say that." I was going to talk him through my moisturising routine but decided it would be incompatible with my image as a tough fighting man.

I know some people would say what I did was unforgiveable. Pretending to serve in the forces is an insult to those who really do.

I don't think I'd inherited any of my dad's contempt for soldiers. I always had a sneaking respect for them. When I'd watched TV documentaries about Army life, I'd seen people rucking through the jungle with forty kilogram bergens. If I tried putting one of those on, I'd be on my back flailing like a turtle. All I can say in my defence is: I was desperate. I saw this job as my only option. I wasn't going to be accepted by admitting I'd been expelled from school for being unreliable and having a smart mouth. I didn't think I was taking too much of a risk, though. There was a possibility Mr Curry would try to contact Corporal Clark for a reference. I hoped the Army would have more important things to do than respond to a hotel manager on behalf of a corporal who didn't exist.

"Do you have much experience of hotels?"

I'd never stayed in a hotel. I wasn't sure my dad had, either. He never went to academic conferences. He believed he could understand his peers perfectly well by reading their work. He didn't need to be in the same room drinking cheap wine with them. I coughed twice and blew my nose to buy some thinking time. "More than you might think. My platoon moved around the country a lot. If we were staying in a town that didn't have a base which could accommodate us, we often stayed in hotels. The arrangement was strictly beds only. We always did our own catering, so I know my way around a hotel kitchen."

"That's excellent. To start with, you won't be spending much time in the kitchen, but in the future, who knows? When can you start?"

"How about this afternoon?"

He shook my hand again. "I look forward to working with you."

I returned to school and went up to the dormitory. I didn't want anyone to know I was leaving until I was well away. I left my school clothes in my locker. Another advantage of my new job was that a uniform was provided. I took my underwear, jeans, t-shirts, and toiletries. I packed one set of pyjamas and left another casually on my bed like I full intended to sleep there. I looked around the place for a last time without regret. I felt more nostalgia as I made a final trip to my toilet bolt hole. It was small, cramped, and didn't always smell too good, but it had been a place to hide. I packed my music papers into my bag. I was heading towards the side gate when I saw Mr Wilson. I'd done my best to avoid him but now I wanted him to see me. He was torn between asking where I was going and commenting on my hair, but I got in first. "Ever get your exhaust fixed?" I asked him. "Must have been expensive. Where did you find the bread?"

I didn't see his reaction. I walked out of the school and never went back. At least I left with a smile on my face.

# CHAPTER EIGHTEEN

**A**RRIVING BACK AT THE HOTEL, I went up to the reception desk again. "I'm starting work here today."

A different receptionist in an identical uniform looked at me sternly. "This entrance is for guests only."

I went into the courtyard, with a sudden feeling work might not be much better than school. Passing one of the doors, I was hit by a blast of air—a mix of cheap meat, overcooked vegetables, and strong detergent. The smell reminded me too much of my first day at school. I had an urge to run, but nowhere to go. I figured the smell came from the kitchen and this wasn't an area frequented by the guests. It followed it must be a staff area. I walked past the kitchen. People in sweat-drenched paper hats heaved around huge metal trays filled with cuts of meat and sliced vegetables.

Past the kitchen, I found a staff room. There was a table up against one wall with a kettle and mugs on it. Old settees and chairs were scattered round the room. People aged between seventeen and sixty-five lounged about, reading the paper, smoking, drinking tea, chatting. They were dressed according to their jobs. Those who worked in the kitchen wore checked trousers and white double-breasted jackets with brown and red stains down the front. They were encouraged to operate behind the scenes, keeping out of sight. The waiters, waitresses, and receptionists who met the guests were dressed in white shirt with black bow tie and waistcoat. There were those like me who worked in the guests' rooms. It wasn't our job to interact with the public, but it would inevitably happen. We wore black trousers, white shirt, and tie of any colour, but with a 'not too gaudy' stipulation.

I didn't know any of this at the time. All I saw was a room full of strange faces. "Strength at the back is the most important thing," said one.

"You reckon it's more important than dominance in the air?" asked another.

"What are you talking about?" demanded a third. "A guy up front who can stick it in the back of the net is what you need. Everything else is just icing on the cake."

I had the heavy-chested feeling I wasn't going to fit in here, either. I knew they were talking about football. I also knew I had nothing to contribute to this conversation.

One of them looked at me curiously but without hostility. "Who are you?" he asked.

"Hello, I'm the new boy."

"You have my sympathy," said a white-haired man in the corner.

"Run for the hills," added another.

I was already thinking along these lines but smiled politely. "What do I do? Where do I go?"

There was some shrugging. "No idea, mate."

"Have a brew. Always a good way to start."

Thanks to my dad's preferences, there was always coffee in the house when I was growing up. We were the only house in Britain with no tea. I didn't want to make my first cup in front of my new colleagues in case I did something wrong. There was a noticeboard on the wall. I had a look to see if it offered any clues about what I was supposed to do.

Someone tapped me on the shoulder. "Hello, my name's Jen. I'm your mum." That sounded like a novel experience. I turned to see a girl, a couple of years older than me. The top of her head was at the same level as my chin, which made her about five foot two. She had reddish-brown hair flowing down to the small of her back, blue eyes, and a smiling, freckly face. Her broad shoulders were needed to support her ample chest. The shirt and tie gave her an Annie Hall look, which became her well. "Mr Curry was looking for someone to train you and I drew the short straw. First of all, know that I commit unspeakable acts of violence against anyone who calls me Jenny. Come on, we need to get you kitted out." She took me into a room where rows of black trousers and white shirts were hung up. She held a pair of trousers against my waist and decided they were the right length. "Change in the toilets. If I see you in your pants, I might not be able to control myself. Put your civvies in this bag." The work trousers crackled as I put them on. The hairs on my legs rose and poked through the nylon. The white shirt was too big, but if I tucked it in and rolled up the sleeves, I didn't look too ridiculous. I unlocked the toilet door and stepped outside in my new work attire. Jen looked me up and down with a little smile. "Modelling this season's fashions."

There was a bank of pigeonholes and a row of pegs outside the staff room. Jen pulled a sheet of paper from one of the holes. Taking one of the master keys from its peg, she walked towards the service lift. "Enjoy today," she said, waving the paper at me. "The last time you *don't* have one of these to your name." The lift arrived. It was small and rickety with a bare metal interior. I had to stand close to Jen, during which time I discovered she smelled of a strong, flowery perfume, which made me feel pleasantly dizzy. As we rode up to the third floor, she showed me the list of numbers on the paper. "These are the rooms allocated to each bedder. Beside each room number, it says 'IR' or 'CO', which means 'in residence' or 'checked out.' Let's start with a CO." We stepped out of the lift and walked along the corridor. Stopping in front of one of the doors, Jen turned to me. "I should warn you we never know what we'll find on the other side of the door. It could be fine, or it might be the worst thing you've ever seen. Most people are okay. They arrive, they sleep, they move on. Others take the rock star approach to staying in a hotel."

"Channelling the spirit of Keith Moon?" I suggested.

"Who?"

"That's right, from The Who."

She frowned. "Your words sound like they *should* mean something."

I saw I had as much to teach her as she me. That was for another time, though. "One thing, Jen," I asked. "What am I?"

"You really want me to tell you?"

"Mr Curry didn't tell me what my job title is. You used the word 'bedder' a minute ago."

"Officially, we're general assistants, but so are the waiters and the guys who serve behind the bar. To distinguish ourselves from that rabble, we call ourselves bedders. Now, are you ready to be the best bedder you can be? Watch and learn."

She opened the door and peeped in cautiously as if fearing there'd be blood—or worse—dripping from the ceiling. Looking relieved, she beckoned me to follow her. The first thing she went for was the pound coin laid at the end of the bed. She pocketed it. "I can afford to eat for another day. If there's any money left on the bed or the desk, you can assume it's for you. This isn't the sort of place that attracts millionaires so don't expect to buy a new car with the tips. If you're lucky, you'll make enough for a beer. Money found anywhere else after the guest has checked out is a matter for your own conscience. I reckon anything up to a fiver is fair game and it goes in my pocket. Any more, I take it to lost property. I'm not as honest as the day is long, but I'm good for most of the morning. There's a competition between all of us bedders to see who can find the strangest thing left behind in a room, with a prize given out at the staff Christmas party. The grail is to find a baby. No one's managed it yet, but who knows, you might be the chosen one. Failing that, any evidence of crime or sexual deviance is much sought-after. Find a safe-cracking kit or a gimp mask and you're well on the way to the prize. All the rooms have a Bible in the bedside drawer. Always check them. When guests are bored and drunk, they sometimes rewrite the sacred text. The most common one is crossing out the word 'not' and creating divine injunctions to steal and commit adultery. Guests have been known to leave watches and suits in their rooms. Anything valuable also goes to lost property. Will someone come back for a ratty old pair of trainers with a hole in the toe? Probably not, so they can go in the bin. No one's going to miss a half-empty bottle of shampoo, so you can take it back to your room and save yourself a bit of money. You might smell of camellias for a few weeks, but we don't judge. Most of the job is cleaning up. People staying in a strange town drink too much, take a puff of something illegal, and spend a night in bed with the wife—not necessarily their own. Any substance that can emerge from the human body will be found in hotel rooms. My advice is: don't think about it; squirt bleach on it and wipe it up."

Jen and I spent two hours going to all the rooms on her list. We didn't find any babies or excessive amounts of human effluent. I helped more each time. By the last room, she stood back and watched her protégé at work. She looked satisfied I could survive in the wild. "Let me show you to your quarters."

It was a shock to move from the guest rooms into the part the public never saw. It wasn't a five-star hotel, so there were no chandeliers or marble floors, but the corridors between the guest rooms had soft green carpets. The paintings on the walls were sub-Pollock abstracts. Stepping through the door marked Staff Only, we found black linoleum curling up at the corners and cream paint peeling off the walls.

Jen showed me a room with floor to ceiling white tiles. Many of them were cracked and the grouting was black with mould. This didn't bother me. It was an individual toilet and shower room with a lock on the door. I could scrub myself clean every day away from prying eyes. She gave me the key to room twenty-nine. "I'll let you take possession." I opened the door, and we went in. The room was ten feet by six with a bed, a table, and a wardrobe. The floorboards and light bulb were both bare. I looked around for a moment. She put her hand on my arm. "Come on, it's not so bad."

She'd misinterpreted the tears running down my face. I didn't care how small or spartan it was. I had a bolt hole again.

# CHAPTER NINETEEN

ABDUL'S WORK ETHIC MUST HAVE RUBBED OFF ON me because I became a respectable member of the hotel's team. I showed up for my shift on time, clean and reasonably sober. I did a good job. I was polite to the guests. What would Mr Wilson have thought if he'd seen me?

Check-in started at midday, so all the rooms needed to be ready for the guests by a quarter to twelve at the latest. Afterwards, we went to the break room for a cup of tea. Mr Curry debriefed us on anything we needed to know. I liked him. He wasn't like the teachers at school: he was in a position of authority but didn't relish the power. He took the view that we had a job to do and would work together to get it done.

Initially, I found it difficult to talk to my fellow bedders. Once again, video nasties came to my rescue. Although they were now banned, they were still part of the consciousness. A certain status was accorded to those who had seen these films in the most nonchalant manner. "I watched *Cannibal Ferox* while I was having my tea one day."

"I woke up one morning with a raging hangover. I still sat through *I Spit On Your Grave*."

I couldn't run any screenings, but I could talk about them. Any time there was a lull in conversation, I threw in another title, which usually started a discussion of some sort.

I was finished shortly after twelve. Although I enjoyed the job, I didn't want to do it forever. I could imagine the withering look on my dad's face when I told him I cleaned hotel rooms for a living. He wasn't a snob in the traditional sense. He had great respect for anyone from a poor background who fought his way to university. He was an intellectual snob. For him, people were essentially brains. The body was just a bag to carry the brain around in. He despised people who didn't use the brains they'd been given. In his ideal world, all manual jobs would be done by machines, leaving people free to explore ideas, be creative, and do all the things machines could never do—or, at least, not as well as people could. The local college of further education was a fifteen-minute walk from the hotel. I went there after my shift one Monday in September, a couple of weeks before the start of a new term. On the way, I had to formulate another plan. Some of the guys at school had been preparing their university applications. The teachers had hinted ominously about what would happen if they wrote someone a bad reference. The last thing I wanted was the college contacting the school to see if they would recommend me as a good student.

I went into another reception area and asked to speak to the person in charge of part-time courses. As I sat and waited, I wondered again what the parents had been paying for at school. The college was free to all students, but the chairs in reception had all their stuffing still inside them. The magazines fanned out on the table were less than five years old. "Hello, I'm Bianca," said a voice. I looked up and saw a woman in her forties striding towards me with long black hair and a green silk scarf billowing behind her.

I stood up and held out my hand. "Eye ya doohan?" I asked, in the American accent I'd learned from watching movies about the Mafia.

She took me into a little room. "What can we do for you?"

I found it hard to keep the accent up so toned it down a little. "I'm an English guy," I explained, "but my dad has a job teaching at an American university." So far, so true. "I've been at high school in Michigan. You may notice a twang in my accent."

She smiled. "I thought it sounded a bit . . . unusual."

"Now I'm back here, I'd like to go to an English university. Some of them are a bit funny about accepting high school diplomas."

She frowned. "Really? I thought most places accepted international qualifications."

I was afraid I'd said the wrong thing but continued, "The admissions officer I spoke to told me they generally prefer English qualifications. So . . . here I am."

I had a feeling my story would fall apart if she probed any further, but she said, "I'm sure we can help you."

The difference between school and college was extraordinary. I was required to go to lessons and do the homework and . . . nothing else! No one asked me to play cricket or attend assemblies. The teachers were there because of their interest in the subject and in education. They weren't there to exert power over children. At school, knowledge was something which had to be forced into pupils with the threat of punishment. The teachers at college knew we wouldn't be there unless we wanted to be. They concentrated on making the subject interesting and trusted learning would happen automatically.

Back at the hotel, Jen did random checks on the rooms I'd serviced and offered hints. I never had the feeling she enjoyed the little bit of power she had over me. She wanted to help me be good at my job. The strange thing was she also spent time with me when she didn't have to. She often sat next to me at lunchtime or during a coffee break. If I hadn't known better, I'd have thought she liked me.

After the hotel restaurant closed, one of the chefs would come to the door of the break room and shout, "Feeding time!" We could help ourselves to anything the guests hadn't eaten.

At one feeding time, I was trying to break through the blackened cheese crust of a lasagne when Jen sat down next to me. "Mr Curry told me you came here after a distinguished military career of leading your troops into battle against overwhelming odds. I'm going to say that's bullshit. Don't worry. I won't tell anyone, but you can be honest with me. After all, I am your mum."

"What gave it away?" I asked.

"I've got a couple of cousins in the Army. It's not like they're at attention all the time but they stand a bit straighter than everyone else. You amble about the place all round-shouldered with your head poking forward like a turtle's. Ironing perfect creases into every item of clothing is drilled into soldiers until it becomes second nature." Looking me up and down, she shook her head. "That shirt would not pass muster. You have ironed it, but not very well." She put her hand under the table and patted my belly. I was eating better at the hotel than I had at Abdul's and the job involved a certain amount of going up and down stairs, so my belly had reduced, but it was still there. "Don't get me wrong. I think you look okay." I took a moment to appreciate this. It was the most gushing compliment I'd ever received from a woman. "I'm not sure you're trained to peak fitness and ready for combat at a moment's notice."

I didn't want to shout about lying in my interview in case I was kicked out of the job, so I deflected the conversation. "You seem smart."

"Thank you. Sometimes I go whole days without drooling over myself."

"Sorry if that sounded patronising."

"I know you didn't mean it. It just comes naturally to you."

"How did you end up here?"

"I love reading, so I signed up to do English at college. The trouble was I always found something more interesting to read than anything on the course. When I read a great book, I *feel* it's great rather than thinking it. Writing essays was tough because no one wanted to hear a story made my fingertips tingle or felt like cinnamon bubbling in my stomach."

On Friday afternoons, we lined up outside the operations manager's office to receive our wages. He handed us each an envelope, which had a staple through the middle, holding the banknotes in place. We were supposed to open the envelope carefully and count the money. If we had any queries, we had to show the operations manager the staple still in situ or he refused to listen. Some of the guys couldn't be bothered and just ripped the envelope open. On Friday evenings, a lot of us did what Jen called wage recycling. The hotel gave us money. We went to the hotel bar and gave it back. I was saving up for a new cassette player, so I normally spent the evening in my room. Jen complained my behaviour was too monastic and ordered me to come out and enjoy myself. She sat with me in the corner, and we chatted. Inevitably, I asked her the question, "How many video nasties have you seen?"

She rolled her eyes. "What is it with you and those sodding films?"

"They saved my life." I was halfway through telling her the story when she got bored and kissed me to shut me up. She stood up, took me by the hand and led me to the service lift. I immediately prepared myself for disappointment, but at the same time thought there was a real possibility I was about to take one small step for man. I was faced with a dilemma. If she had decided in a moment of madness to have sex with me, I'd better seize the opportunity before it passed. Equally, I didn't want her to be so appalled by my body she'd never speak to me again. Jen had a room on the floor below mine. As we arrived at her door, I saw the short staircase leading to the floor where my room was. "Back in a second," I said. I ran up the stairs, ripping off my clothes as I went. For once, I didn't care if anyone else saw me. I grabbed all the toiletries I could find and dived into the shower room. It took me less than a minute to shower, wash my hair, dry myself, and douse myself with half a pint of deodorant and cologne. Putting my clothes back on, I ran back down the stairs. After taking a moment to get my breath back, I knocked on Jen's door. I assumed the nonchalant expression of someone who did this sort of thing all the time.

Jen opened the door for me and sat down on the bed. I sat next to her. With no personal experience of what to do, I had to fall back on what I'd seen in films. This was one time when video nasties were no use. The porn I'd seen didn't help much, either. I couldn't ask Jen to climb up a black plastic telephone in a red swimsuit. Fortunately, I'd seen enough romantic comedies and steamy thrillers to have some idea. Many of the sex scenes involved the man slowly removing the woman's clothes and kissing every inch of flesh as it was exposed. I started doing that and, judging by the appreciative little noises Jen made, it went well.

She reached behind her back to unhook her bra. I hadn't appreciated the extent to which large breasts wander about the place. As she lay down on the bed, her right breast migrated to her armpit while the left one tried to escape down her side.

At this point, I thought it best to confess. "To tell you the truth, Jen, I don't have too much experience in this area."

She smiled. "And I thought I was just one more in your list of conquests. I guessed as much, sweetie. Don't worry. I trained you how to service rooms. I'll train you how to service me too. Follow my lead. You can stop at any point to ask directions."

I'd read that something called foreplay is much beloved among women, and it seemed a hard thing to do wrong. Every time a body part is revealed, rhapsodise like it's the Taj Mahal by moonlight. I did this for about twenty minutes. No matter how good the support act is, sooner or later it must yield to the main event of the evening. Clambering on top of her, I expected it to be like a heat-seeking missile efficiently finding its target. I discovered it was more like trying to thread a needle when you're lying on top of it. Fortunately, she came to my rescue and threaded the needle for me.

Considering it was my first time, I don't think I did too badly. I flatter myself I was good in bed simply by paying attention. When

Jen made pleased-sounding moans, I kept on doing the same thing. If a look of boredom or annoyance flashed across her face even for half a second, I mixed it up and tried something else. After fifteen minutes, she was satisfied or good at acting—I never asked because I didn't want to know. As for me, I felt the same as when I had my first glass of beer. I liked it but couldn't quite see why everyone raved about it so much. I was also sure I wanted to try it again. There seemed an obvious way of maximising my chances of being asked back. "So . . ." I began tentatively, "are we . . . an item now?"

She laughed. "An item? How delightfully old-fashioned. You might as well ask if we're walking out together." She paused for a moment. "Yes, okay, why not?"

It wasn't the most passionate declaration of love. Juliet talking about Romeo would have been more eloquent, but it was enough for me. I began the lengthy foreplay process all over again.

We started spending all our time together except when we were working or I was at college. She had an old green Fiat in the staff car park. We would climb in and drive out to a nearby river or rural path. I discovered being in the countryside wasn't all bad. She also took me to staff social events in and around the hotel. I played bingo for the first and last time in my life. I gave a suitably stuttering performance of 'My Generation' at a karaoke evening. Mostly, though, we were either in her room or mine. I had my history books. She had her novels by Arthur Conan Doyle and H. G. Wells. We also had music. Her tastes were about ten years ahead of mine. She loved The Damned, The Clash, and The Stranglers. She was happy to give my music a day in court and we found a lot to like in each other's collections. My mother's records didn't go beyond 1970, so I'd never listened to much punk. I discovered much of it was The Who or The Kinks speeded up. The Stranglers were essentially The Doors with a heavier bass and a singer who was more world-weary than stoned. The Damned even had a song about video nasties, which became a favourite from the first time I heard it. Often, Jen and I didn't talk for a while, but it was nice to have someone to share my bolt hole with. We were young and excitable. It was never long before one of us rolled onto the other and we lost interest in what we were reading.

It cleared up the question of my sexuality. I discovered I was heterosexual, within the strict meaning of the word. I was attracted to things that were different from me. I know some guys are into bottoms or feet, but I had a bottom and feet of my own and didn't think much of them. I was intrigued by Jen's breasts. My own were inconsequential pink buttons. Hers had a pleasing size, shape, and heaviness. It was the late 1980s, when pubic hair was still legal, and I enjoyed exploring the undergrowth in search of hidden valleys and promontories. The most surprising thing was she didn't seem revolted by my body. I had hoped to examine every inch of hers, flip the light off, then get undressed myself without her having to see anything. It turned out this wasn't necessary. Strangely, she seemed to find my snowy white body appealing. "One second in the sun and you'd be a pile of ashes. My sexy vampire." I'd never been called sexy before. I liked it.

I also liked that she stopped calling herself my mum after we started sleeping together.

# CHAPTER TWENTY

I WORKED HARD AT COLLEGE. The history lecturer, Mrs Holmes, saw me as a fellow enthusiast and took me under her wing. Our class began at seven in the evening, and she had her tea in the canteen at six. Her favourite meal was a pork chop with mashed potatoes and peas. The catering manager had a little crush on her and prepared this for her every day regardless of what was on the menu. She was happy for me to sit opposite her while we talked about my latest essay. Tall and plump with dyed blonde hair, which spiked up whether she wanted it to or not, she dressed in thick sweaters and shapeless slacks. Her soft voice and educated turn of phrase meant it was always a shock when she threw something into the discussion like, "Your suggestion Mussolini might have been a reincarnation of Caligula is utter bollocks," or, "You went on a bit of a wank about SS insignia. You don't want the examiner thinking you're a crypto-Nazi."

One evening, as we batted ideas back and forth, she gave me a thoughtful look. "Do you know something, poppet? I think you could survive a Cambridge supervision." I wasn't sure what this was. She explained, "You might be able to sit in a room for an hour a week and do some verbal fencing with one of the world's leading historians."

This sounded interesting so we agreed I'd apply to read history at Cambridge. I went to open days and looked round some of the colleges. The ancient ones were impressive pieces of architecture but were better from the outside. Once inside, I noticed some of the radiators didn't work and the window frames had gaps in them. I could imagine the Fenland cold and damp oozing into my bedroom on a winter's night. In the end, I decided to apply to a college younger than me. It didn't have a scholarly tradition dating back to the thirteenth century, but it was warm and dry, which was more important to me at the time. The exterior was redbrick American gothic. The inside resembled a private health clinic with long white corridors, a soothing hush, and people moving about calmly but purposefully.

I was told to wait in the combination room before my interview. I wanted to look like I belonged there, so I didn't let on I had no idea what a combination room was. It turned out to be a plushier version of the quiet room at school. It was a place where members of the college sat around, chatting, or reading the paper. A couple of them took the time to talk to me. When I admitted to working in a hotel, they didn't smirk at the jumped-up housekeeper who wanted to join their intellectual circle. They'd all done a variety of jobs, some of them worse than mine, but they'd found a safe haven in the college. This might be my ultimate bolt hole. The people were nice. The room smelled pleasantly of new carpet and fresh coffee. I felt at home.

Somebody went off to find one of the history students and came back with a guy called Dave. He looked a bit of a thug with his short hair and sturdy boots but turned out to be helpful. Sitting down next to me, he told me what would impress the history fellow who was going to interview me. I was a bit worried as we talked. The interviewer was called Dr Campbell and his main interest was trade in the medieval world. I racked my mind for anything vaguely sensible I could say on this topic. Dave reassured me Dr Campbell was a reasonable man who would want me to do well and wouldn't throw me too many curve balls.

A white-haired man with Lennon glasses and a grey suit opened the door and beckoned to me. "Good luck," said Dave, and started off.

"What have you been telling him, Dave?" asked Dr Campbell, with a grin.

"Only the good stuff, Pete, you know me."

I was surprised at the way they spoke. I'd assumed Cambridge dons were addressed as "learned and distinguished professor." I liked the friendly banter between them. Suddenly, Dr Campbell, or Pete, was more human and less threatening. He took me into a small room and offered me a cigarette, which I turned down. Lighting his own, he said, "You can forget what Dave told you. It's generally a good idea to ignore everything Dave says. I'm not going to ask you about history. Mrs Holmes has told me what I need to know there. I want you to think on your feet, but you can stay sitting down. You're shipwrecked and on a small rowing boat with five other people. There's no food and no prospect of being rescued any time soon. One of the men dies. Do you eat him?"

"What's he wearing?" I asked.

His eyebrows flickered. He hadn't expected that question. He took a thoughtful drag on his cigarette. "It's chilly on the boat, so he's wearing long trousers and a thick sweater."

"In that case, I'd remove a length of wool from his sweater. I'd find some sharp object which I'd use to cut away a small cube of the poor chap's flesh. After tying the latter to the former, I'd dangle the length of wool over the side of the boat and try to catch some fish. It's a little more disrespect than I'd like to show a dead body but stops short of outright cannibalism."

I was hoping he'd quiz me further on my views about cannibalism, allowing me to steer the conversation towards video nasties.

At the end of the interview, he said, "You think a little differently from other people." I'd already worked that out. "I like it, so get an A in history A-level, try not to make too embarrassing a mess of the other two, and there'll be a room waiting for you here in October."

# CHAPTER TWENTY-ONE

O N THE DAY THE RESULTS CAME OUT, Mrs Holmes gathered me into her copious bosom. "Well done, poppet." I knew everything was going to be all right even before I opened the envelope.

I was sad to be leaving work. I'd met some nice people there. I was grateful to the hotel for giving me a place where I could piece myself back together and undo some of the damage done by the school. Jen drove me the two hours to Cambridge. I could have taken the train, but she said it would give us a chance to talk. In fact, we didn't say much. When we arrived, the man in the Porters' Lodge asked her if she was a new student. I wished it were the case. It would have been so great to stride into the new college with a readymade support bubble. The man gave me the key to my room and pointed me to the lift. Jen helped me unpack my things and we sat on my new bed, unsure whether to have sex or not. In the end, we both wordlessly decided it would make parting more difficult. We hugged. I thanked her for everything. She left me to it.

I had yet another bolt hole. It wasn't so different from my room in the hotel with a bed, desk, chair, and basin. If I wanted a toilet or bath, I had to walk on down the hall.

On my way in, I'd picked up a large induction pack from my pigeonhole. It included the list of all the getting-to-know-you events in the first week. I went along to these and spent most of my time standing on the outskirts of conversations, smiling and nodding. What I missed most about Jen was having someone who'd *choose* to hang with me. It took me a while to find other people like that.

Jen and I wrote to each other for a couple of months after I started at university. We made plans she'd come and visit once I had my feet under the table and knew how things worked. They do say no relationship survives one or both parties going off to university. It was only a matter of time before one of us found someone else. She beat me to it. In a letter which appeared in my pigeonhole one morning, she told me, 'I'm sure by now you're up to your neck in brilliant intellectual women who talk dirty to you in Latin, so you'll be glad to get rid of this simple serving wench. A few weeks ago, Mr Curry asked me to take a new guy under my wing and, as you know, sleeping with me is an important part of the training process. Seriously, though, he's a nice guy and I want to see how things go with him. I loved the time I spent with you. Have a wonderful life and think of me from time to time as you scale the heights of academia.'

I was sad, obviously. I'll always be grateful to her. She played a big part in helping me to recover from school. Her willingness to get naked with me and fool around suggested my body wasn't completely repulsive. More than that, her wanting to spend time with me reassured me I wasn't a weirdo who made everyone around me uncomfortable. This gave me the confidence to go to lunch at college. Before, I'd have had a chocolate bar in my room. The college dining hall was long and narrow with a church-like vaulted ceiling. Dave was sitting with the other history students at the end of one of the tables. He waved me over. The others didn't acknowledge me when I sat down as they were deep in discussion about the relationship between Hitler and Mussolini. "Why would Hitler divert resources to prop up someone who was clearly doomed?"

"Because they were friends?"

"I'm not sure they liked each other much as people."

"Hitler didn't have too many qualms about throwing his friends under a bus when it suited him."

"Maybe he thought he needed an ally, even if the ally was a liability."

"The man who believed he could rule the world single-handed also thought he needed an ally?"

I waited until a lull in the conversation and launched into the best take I could manage of my dad's impersonation of Mussolini speaking German. At first, they frowned, wondering what the hell I was doing. As they cottoned on, the laughter started. "That was brilliant," said one of them. The others nodded with approval. I became one of the gang, and didn't even need to talk about video nasties to do it.

After lunch, I went to the office and asked for some paper and envelopes headed with the college coat of arms. I had a story prepared about needing to prove my residence in the college to the local council which was funding my studies. It included a number of colourful details about the officious bureaucrat I had to deal with. The college secretary asked me how many I wanted and handed them over with no questions.

I had an envelope with the insignia of an academic institution on it. I thought there was a chance my dad would open it, so I sat down and wrote to him.

Lisa Burke

IT ALL WENT WRONG WHEN I was sent to a Quaker school. The teachers' approach was, "We think you're shit—prove us wrong," which didn't seem very Quakerly. I believed them, didn't prove them wrong, and left school convinced I couldn't do anything. I spent the next seven years trying to piece myself back together, working as a barman and short-order chef, teaching English, French, and guitar. I also took college courses and finally got into the University of Cambridge. I spent three happy years there, writing comedy sketches and articles for the university paper. I emerged with a fairly respectable degree in philosophy, a long-term girlfriend, and a contract to write a book about Joe Orton. The book deal was great, but wasn't going to make a huge amount of money, so I spent a few years training and managing people at Yellow Pages. As Google took over from Yellow Pages as the source of all knowledge, I saw my job wasn't going to last. After a year teaching English in Paris, I moved back to Reading, where I live with my wife and dog. I divide my time between teaching French people over the phone and writing books.

www.ingramcontent.com/pod-product-compliance
Lightning Source LLC
Chambersburg PA
CBHW011520100726
47899CB00010BD/3450

* 9 7 8 1 6 8 4 9 2 1 8 5 0 *